# Billionaire BROKE Girls

A Story of Betrayal, Brokenness, and Bad Business

# Billionaire BROKE Girls

## SHARAIN HEMINGWAY

*Author of All 4 Love*

Published by Mynd Matters Publishing
2690 Cobb Parkway SE
Ste A5-375
Smyrna, GA 30080
www.myndmatterspublishing.com

ISBN: 978-1-963874-63-1 (pbk)
ISBN: 978-1-963874-64-8 (hdcv)
e-ISBN: 978-1-963874-65-5 (eBook)

FIRST EDITION

*"God doesn't waste pain. He repurposes it for power."*
—Unknown


To my mother, my muse,
you planted seeds of faith in barren seasons and never stopped praying
for my return to purpose. Your quiet strength taught me that broken
women still build altars. This is for you.

To the women I've wept with, worked beside, and warred for, the ones
who know the weight of silent battles and smiling through storms.
*Billionaire Broke Girls* is your inheritance.

To the girls who lost everything chasing validation...and to the queens
who rose from the ruins anyway, you are the reason I wrote this. You
are the movement.

This isn't just a story. It's a spiritual uprising. Let's rise together.

With love,

**Sharain**

# Contents

## PART V: THE BIRTH

# Prologue

The humid weight of the South clung to Autumn's skin like sweat and secrets. The front porch of her grandmother's house, once a sacred space of sweet tea and Sunday stories, now simmered with tension thick enough to choke on. This wasn't just a house. It was a memory. It was history. But at present, it was the site of war.

"You are a grandmother!" Autumn's voice cracked through the air like thunder.

"This is MY MOTHER'S HOUSE!" Aretha bellowed, her rage hot and unfiltered.

The words stung, not because they were new, but because they'd been said before—quietly, bitterly, in whispers over Sunday dinners, in side-eyes at funerals, in forced hugs at family reunions. This argument had been brewing for decades.

Autumn's patience snapped like a dry twig.

"I'm not about to keep going back and forth with you, Auntie. Yeah, this might be your mother's house. But this," she motioned to the weathered walls, the soft creak of the old floorboards, the very soul of the home, "is my grandmother's home."

The difference mattered. To Autumn, it always had.

Her voice dropped low, sharp with grief and fire.

"You're a grandmother. Act like it. I'm not about to stand here and let you scream in my face while you sleep on her couch like some angry squatter. Go to hell, or better yet, build a home so your grandkids can visit their grandmother like I'm trying to visit mine."

That was the truth under the wound: Aretha had never built anything of her own, not really. She had inherited bitterness, not legacy. She carried her childhood grudges like a purse, always over her shoulder, ready to unzip.

Brooklyn, Autumn's big cousin, stepped in, gently repositioning their grandmother's walker as a quiet but firm barrier between the fury in front of them and the fragile legacy behind them.

"I'm calling the police and getting you out of here!" Aretha shrieked, pointing a trembling finger, mascara smudged from heat and emotion.

Autumn tilted her head, unbothered.

"Please. Use my phone."

Because the truth? Autumn wasn't afraid of the police. She was afraid of repeating history. Of becoming the woman who never healed. The woman who held power but no peace.

"Stop this..." came a cracked whisper.

Autumn turned around.

There, gripping her arm with frail determination, stood Rose, Autumn's 105-year-old grandmother, her constant. Her voice was so weak it could've been mistaken for a cough, but her eyes burned with clarity.

"Don't," Rose rasped. "I want to keep the peace."

Autumn's fire dimmed for a beat. But only a beat.

"Granny, you need to tell her. She's out of control. If she calls the cops..." Autumn hesitated, lowering her voice. "I'll have to tell them everything."

Buried in that sentence was a graveyard full of secrets. Secrets about deeds signed under false names. About checks written to cover addictions. About who really kept the lights on when Aretha left the mortgage unpaid for five months straight. Secrets about what Rose had covered to keep her family's name out of court.

It was a bluff...mostly.

There were still some of Granny's truths, buried deep like family silver, that neither of them would ever speak aloud. Not to the police. Not to preachers. Not even to each other.

"Just go home," Rose pleaded softly. "We'll talk when you get back from the funeral."

The words sank into Autumn's chest like stones. Go home? Where was home now?

Not Charlotte, where Sam's ghost still lingered in business meetings and betrayal. Not this porch, where family blood boiled over like unprayed prayers.

This house, this dirt road, this legacy built on hand-me-downs and held-in screams, didn't feel like hers anymore. It felt like haunted land. A kingdom with no crown. A battlefield dressed up like a memory.

Autumn looked around one last time, her silence louder than any goodbye.

She didn't slam the door.

She didn't curse or cry.

She just walked away, praying the porch wouldn't collapse under the weight of everything left unsaid.

As her feet crunched the gravel drive, a single thought pulsed in her mind.

*I finally understand why Terri wanted to sell Big Momma's house in Soul Food.*

She exhaled. Her prayer was not for justice or even peace, but for mercy.

"God forgive them," she whispered, "for they know not what they do. Amen."

And just like that, she left Aretha behind. Until they would face each other again. No more screaming. No apology. Just silence, like the kind that settles after a storm. Because sometimes, the loudest part of a family isn't the fight. It's the stillness that follows.

* * *

The funeral was held at Monroe Manor, the ancestral estate that sat like a crown jewel just outside the city limits of Charlotte. Though it hadn't functioned as a full-time residence in months, the manor remained a symbol, part myth, part mausoleum, of the Monroe family's reach, power, and unresolved history.

On that day, the sprawling grounds were hushed. The magnolias bloomed in defiant, fragrant tribute. Somewhere beneath their roots, old secrets stirred. Here, under the warm glow of golden light, friends and family gathered to honor Samantha Monroe—mentor, mogul, and a woman whose life had been as complex as the estate itself. The room was both intimate and expansive, a fitting stage for a farewell that felt too soon and yet inevitable.

Inside, crystal chandeliers threw fractured light across waxed mahogany floors. The portraits of stern-faced women in corsets, men with eyes like Caleb, Samantha's sole heir, watched from the walls, bearing silent witness to yet another chapter of family legacy folding in on itself.

Guests arrived in reverent clusters, their footsteps echoing as they moved through the marble foyer and into the grand ballroom, a space typically reserved for galas, political fundraisers, and once, Samantha Monroe's fiftieth birthday. Now it cradled a casket and the weight of a community unsure of how to mourn someone they never fully knew.

The ballroom didn't feel like a place of grief. It shimmered like a coronation. The color palette, per Sam's request, was hot pink and apple green, her beloved sorority hues. The floral arrangements spiraled toward the ceiling. String quartets filled the air with a reimagined "I Believe I Can Fly," each note feathered in aching nostalgia.

Autumn Brees James stood still just beyond the archway, heels clicking against marble. Her black dress felt too muted in the room's unrepentant glamour. Still, she was there, chosen, whether by God, fate, or Samantha's final whim.

A gentle hand tugged her from her daze.

"Drink this," Brooklyn said, slipping her a green tea shot and a knowing wink. "It's not prayer oil, but it helps."

Autumn chuckled, thankful her cousin had come.

"I don't know why she asked me to speak," she confessed, voice low.

Brooklyn's eyes softened. "Because you're the only one who would tell the truth and still mean it."

Before Autumn could reply, a voice she hadn't heard in nearly a year came from behind.

"Hey, Autumn."

Serenity Sanders.

Her friend. Her prayer warrior. Her mirror. She reached out, offering three taps on Autumn's wrist, their silent code for *you're not alone.*

Autumn tried to inhale, but the room was heavy with memory. Perfume, politics, and unspoken debts. Her gaze drifted over the crowd of preachers, professors, and protégés. People who once loved Samantha. People who still feared her.

Then she saw her. Natalie Sullivan, framed in light like a portrait, comes alive. She'd once idolized Natalie. A mentor. A myth. But now? All she saw was an illusion. Emotional intelligence wrapped in designer lies.

"You're brave," Natalie whispered with a frozen grin. "I wouldn't have dared to speak today."

Autumn didn't answer. Her eyes found the harp instead, where strings spilled a hymn like holy water.

Autumn's attention snapped back as Natalie's minion rambled about the harp's heritage: solid Sitka spruce soundboard, 23-karat gold leaf, French rococo elegance. It was a quarter-million-dollar statement piece meant to distract from the truth.

At the front of the room, a bouquet of black roses rested on the casket. One note, no flourish: —*Rest in peace, J*

Jerald. Samantha's ex-husband. The man who once wrote her poetry and wore heartbreak like a tuxedo. He stood beside the casket in silence. His lips pressed to a prayer only he could hear. Autumn approached hesitantly.

"Did you love her?"

His eyes didn't move.

"More than I could hold. But eventually, you have to close the door that hurts you. Even if the view is beautiful."

Caleb Monroe sat nearby. Jaw tight. Shoulders still. Not a single tear. Not at the wake. Not during the will. Not now.

When the pastor invited loved ones to speak, Caleb rose slowly and reluctantly.

"She was complicated," he began, voice smooth as polished stone. "But she believed in redemption. Sometimes too much."

Autumn flinched. The subtext cut deep.

"She took in people who didn't deserve her," he added, glancing at the front pew.

People murmured. Someone coughed. Someone else said, "Amen," unsure if it was for Caleb or against him.

"She always said purpose doesn't play favorites..." he hesitated. "Even when it should. Rest in peace, mom."

Then he left the mic, leaving a chill in his wake.

Autumn stared after him, heart pounding. It wasn't just grief filling the room now. It was something else.

Serenity leaned over. "You feel that?"

Autumn nodded, eyes locked on Caleb.

"It's not just mourning," she whispered. "It's a warning."

When Autumn stepped to the podium, silence followed like a curtain drop. Even Natalie blinked.

"I am Autumn Brees," she said evenly, "and I was one of Samantha's closest friends and business partners...until I wasn't."

Gasps flickered through the crowd like wind through candlelight.

"I'm not here to canonize her. I'm not here to crucify her, either. I'm here because I know what it means to be raised by someone who saw the world not as it is, but as something to be conquered." She reached down and lifted a worn manila folder.

"She kept one of these on most of you. Notes. Secrets. Leverage. Sam didn't believe in confession. She believed in insurance."

Hazel stood abruptly, snatched her folder, and walked out without a word.

The air shifted again from shock to relief.

"I loved her," Autumn continued. "But I also feared her, and love rooted in fear will never survive the storm." She looked at the crowd and let her voice crack.

"She made me forget to ask if I was okay. If I was happy. If I was safe. She taught me to strive, but not to rest. She taught me to serve, but not to feel." Autumn inhaled.

"But today, I bury not just Sam, but the parts of me that confused achievement with worth. Silence with loyalty. Manipulation with mentorship."

She looked skyward. Not toward Samantha, but toward freedom.

"She had a system of silence. A methodology of manipulation. But we are not concubines. We are not pawns. We are *not* hers anymore."

The ballroom held its breath.

"God," she prayed, "have mercy on every soul under the sound of my voice. Let Samantha Monroe rest and let the rest of us finally rise."

# PART I

## THE ELEVATOR DOWN

# CHAPTER ONE

# The Mirror Lies

Several months after the funeral, Autumn stood inside the mirrored elevator of Park & Madison Consulting, thirty-seven stories above Charlotte. Her Jimmy Choo heels glinted beneath her, like polished armor, reflecting the kind of power she used to wear without question. From this height, the skyline once made her feel invincible. Now, it felt like a glossy postcard from a version of her life that no longer fit.

In the mirrored walls, her reflection appeared pristine: radiant cinnamon skin kissed by sunlight, edges laid with surgical precision, a silk blouse tucked into tailored navy trousers that whispered generational wealth and curated control. She appeared to be a woman who had it all.

But inside? She was quietly imploding.

The brass plaque outside her office still read *Vice President – Strategic Vision,* but today, she wasn't going upstairs. She wasn't preparing for a pitch, a review, or a quarterly war disguised as a team meeting. Today, Autumn was leaving for good.

She pressed the button for the ground floor. Her hand trembled.

*Be focused. Have faith. Walk by every mirror flawlessly.*

That mantra had been her internal drumbeat for over a decade. It got her through boardrooms built like battlegrounds. Through all-white panels where her Black brilliance was either commodified or dismissed. Through veiled threats couched as "mentorship" and compliments that doubled as subtle warnings.

It was more than a motto. It had been her shield. But legends, even legendary Black women, get tired, too. Especially after burying the woman who taught you to perform perfection...and then betrayed everything you believed about yourself.

The elevator dinged softly. No fanfare. No farewell lunch. Just a half-hearted wave from a receptionist scrolling TikTok, and the bitter scent of burnt coffee clinging to the air like unresolved conflict.

Autumn dropped her company ID into the trash.

Not symbolic. Not dramatic. Necessary.

She walked out, her heels echoing across the marble lobby. It wasn't freedom yet, but it was the first real breath of it.

Outside, July heat greeted her like a full-body confrontation—thick, unrelenting, and humid with memory. The noise of the city moved around her as if she were invisible. Executives. Influencers. Hustlers. All chasing the next thing.

She turned instinctively toward the café across the street. *The Violet Rose.* With that, the memory slammed into her.

The café was curated chaos: lavender steam, ambient jazz, and the smell of purpose in the air. Autumn, newly promoted and still glowing from the announcement, sat tucked into a corner booth with her iPad and a rose chai latte. Autumn always wore hope as though it were the latest must-have perfume. Her spreadsheets were gospel, and her calendar was sacred.

Samantha Monroe swept in twenty minutes late, draped in Gucci, smelling like jasmine and unfinished truths. She moved like someone who expected the world to pivot around her. In many ways, it often did.

"Autumn Brees James!" she beamed. "You look like a whole Forbes feature. Sis, don't you dare let these white boys dim your gold."

Autumn laughed, a little shy. Sam had that effect. She saw you, spoke directly to the part of you that longed to be affirmed.

"I just signed the papers. Promotion's official," Autumn said.

Sam snapped her fingers, triumphant. "I *knew* it. You always had that walk. The one that says: *I earned this, and I dare you to take it from me.*" She leaned in, lowering her voice. "But that title? That office? Baby girl, it's a trap. A corner-office cage with a nice view."

Autumn raised an eyebrow. "A cage?"

"Glass ceilings are polite prisons," Sam said with a smirk. "You're a queen playing corporate concubine. Let me show you something."

She reached into her designer tote and pulled out a matte-black folder. Inside was a brand deck, logos, projections, and glossy mock-ups of a platform that promised power, ownership, and freedom.

Autumn's eyes scanned the pages. It looked legit. More than legit, it looked like destiny.

"You trust me, right?" Sam asked, her tone casual but eyes laser-focused.

"Of course," Autumn replied, before thinking twice. "You've always looked out for me."

Sam smiled, too wide. "Then don't overthink it. Faith moves faster than fear. Let's jump."

When the check came, Sam slid it across the table to Autumn with a wink.

"Your treat since you're the one with the corporate coin now."

Autumn paid without protest.

But that moment three years ago was the first red flag, wrapped in praise and dressed up as mentorship. Autumn hadn't seen it for what it was. Not back then.

* * *

## Present Day

The crosswalk light blinked green, snapping her out of the memory. The Violet Rose still stood, prettier than ever. The windows were lined with lavender sprigs and gold-script signs advertising "Organic Matcha" and "Soulful Wi-Fi."

But Autumn didn't step inside. Not this time. Her phone buzzed, indicating a text from her mother: *Sorry I couldn't be there. Hope you're holding up.*

That was it. No call. No visit. No follow-up. Just a sentence full of distance.

Autumn stared at it for a moment before locking her phone. Not angry. Just...done trying to decode the silence. *She's always kept me at arm's length. Like I'm a responsibility, not a daughter.* It was another mantra she never meant to inherit.

Her grip on her handbag tightened. From somewhere nearby, a breeze passed. Lavender and jasmine. It was reminiscent of Samantha. Gone, and still everywhere.

Still inside her planner. Still in the forged contracts her lawyer was unraveling. Still in her nightmares.

Autumn kept walking past the café, past the mirrored windows of boutiques selling lives she no longer envied. In one pane, she caught a glimpse of herself again. Still beautiful. Still flawless. But this time, she didn't smile.

She stared at the woman looking back, and whispered, "You lied to me." The mirror didn't argue.

It never had. Because mirrors don't tell the truth, they just reflect what we've been forced to believe.

And Autumn Brees James? She was finally ready to believe something new.

# CHAPTER TWO

# START with GOD

The room shimmered with sacred expectancy. Linen-draped tables. Gold-rimmed plates. Fresh-cut white roses nestled in tall glass vases. This wasn't just brunch. It was holy ground wrapped in satin and sunlight.

A gathering of mothers, daughters, aunties, mentors, and menders. Generations of Black women dressed in their Sunday best and silent prayers. Heels clicked against polished floors, laughter laced the air like incense, and hope whispered through every corner.

Autumn Brees James stepped through the double doors, late and unannounced. Her Gucci frames sat perfectly on her face, but couldn't hide the tired swell beneath her eyes. She moved like she still belonged in rooms like this. But everything inside her whispered what she didn't want to admit: she didn't. Not anymore.

At the front of the ballroom, the young event hostess beamed behind the mic.

"Ladies," she began, voice glowing, "this brunch has never been just about food. It's about healing. It's about legacy. And today...we are honored, *truly* honored, to welcome a voice who's helped thousands come home to themselves."

The spotlight followed her gaze. "Please welcome, Serenity Annette Sanders." The applause was thunderous.

Autumn winced—part reverence, part regret, because Serenity Sanders wasn't just any speaker. She was *the* speaker. A licensed therapist. A best-selling author. A coach to CEOs and congresswomen. And the *last* woman Autumn expected to see again.

Serenity stepped onto the stage in nude heels and a champagne-colored wrap dress. Her presence was elegant, but weighty, like she wasn't there to perform, but to pour. Autumn shrank into her seat and clapped harder than necessary. A nervous habit. She even gave two awkward thumbs up, as if to say, *I'm fine, everything's fine*, even though nothing inside her confirmed the sentiment.

Two weeks ago, Serenity had left her a voicemail.

"Autumn, I know you're grieving Sam. But some grief is spiritual, not emotional. And if you don't face it, it'll follow you into every new season."

Autumn never called her back. But now, here she was.

Their eyes met across the room, and for a split second, recognition passed between them. Serenity didn't react. She just nodded slightly. Then turned to the mic. No intro music. No fanfare. Just a long, reverent pause just before she spoke.

"Have you ever tried to heal in public," she asked, "while still bleeding in private?"

Silence settled like incense.

"Have you ever held secrets so sacred for others that they became sins against yourself?"

Women shifted in their seats. Some inhaled sharply. Serenity's voice didn't tremble, but her presence carried weight. She didn't pace the stage like a motivational speaker. She moved like a woman who'd buried prayers at the altar and came back to tell the truth.

"Healing isn't pretty. But it's *necessary*." She glanced down, her fingers grazing the edge of her notes. "I've been lied to by people I loved. Betrayed by people I built. I've washed the feet of the same folks who nailed me to a cross. Yet, I chose softness."

A few women released audible sounds of agreement and understanding.

"I used to think Jim Carrey lost his mind in *The Truman Show*," she said with a half-smile. "But then I realized, we're *all* in it. Performing. Smiling. Curating peace while privately panicking."

Autumn's breath caught. Serenity's words weren't just poetic. They were prophetic.

"When you study Scripture," she said, stepping closer to the edge of the stage, "anyone who followed God with integrity was wrecked first."

"David was anointed but abandoned. Moses was chosen but rejected. Jesus was perfect and still crucified."

A murmur rolled through the crowd like thunder in deep water.

"So why," Serenity whispered, "are you chasing applause from a world that crucified your Savior?"

Autumn felt her chest tighten and her lashes dampen. She wasn't sure who she was crying for.

Samantha? Herself? God? All of it? None of it?

Serenity's voice cracked. But she didn't stop.

"You think the breaking disqualifies you. But it *makes* you. The betrayal? The bankruptcy? The heartbreak? It's all part of becoming."

More women nodded. Some closed their eyes. Others opened their palms in quiet agreement.

"Some of us are trying to resurrect *brands*," Serenity said, "when God is trying to resurrect *belief*."

That line hit Autumn like glass to the gut.

Because that was her. She was a woman who knew how to rebuild an empire but had forgotten how to rebuild a soul.

The music swelled. The altar call had come in the form of truth. The hostess returned to the mic, her voice gentler now.

"One last tradition," she said. "If you're seated beside a woman who made you stronger, who saw you through something, stand with her now."

Like a gentle wave, they rose. Mothers and daughters. Best friends and battle buddies. Napkins lifted in the air like small white flags, surrender and strength in one motion. It looked like praise, but it *felt* like revival.

Serenity stood at the center, not flawless, but faithful, not as a brand, but as a balm.

Autumn rose, too. Not for applause but for *truth*. Because in that moment, she realized she didn't just lose Samantha Monroe. She lost the version of herself who thought healing was optional.

She wiped her eyes and then slipped toward the exit. Not because she wasn't moved but because she was *undone*.

# CHAPTER THREE

# Corporate Chains, Designer Pain

The conference room inside Monroe Manor was colder than Autumn remembered. Once Samantha Monroe's sanctuary of polished art, imported rugs, and sweeping southern charm, it now pulsed with something harder, more courtroom than home. Even the chandelier seemed to dim beneath the weight of betrayal.

The polished oak table stretched long and glossy, a cold mirror of power and grief. Lined with lawyers, family members, and silent spectators to the Monroe fallout, it was less about mourning and more about money, legacy, and the secrets death could no longer hide.

Autumn sat beside Hazel and Serenity, her posture poised but her spirit frayed. Brooklyn flanked her left, jaw tight, her loyalty sharper than ever. Across from them, Caleb Monroe lounged in calculated stillness. His stillness unsettled her more than rage would have. His expression was unreadable, calm, detached, like a man watching a house burn from the inside with no intention of saving anyone inside it.

Hazel cleared her throat, tapping a folder with clinical precision.

"We're here to finalize the estate and business arrangements following the passing of Samantha Monroe. There are unresolved contracts, frozen accounts, and active investigations surrounding her business assets."

Autumn tried not to flinch at the mention of "investigations." She caught Caleb's gaze for a fraction of a second. He didn't blink.

Hazel continued, voice even.

"Before we proceed, there's a personal statement Caleb asked to deliver. In full transparency, I advised against it."

Every head turned. Caleb stood slowly.

The room fell into a silence that felt older than all of them.

"I've been quiet for too long," Caleb said, voice low and almost eerily calm. "But the truth about my mother, and about what happened, needs to be spoken, even if no one here wants to hear it."

Autumn's breath hitched.

"She wasn't who you think she was," Caleb said. "And her death? RIP Mom." His lips tightened.

Gasps rippled down the table like dominoes tipping over in slow motion.

He looked directly at Autumn, then quickly looked away.

Autumn didn't flinch. But inside, something cracked.

This wasn't just a settlement meeting. It was the reckoning. This was the unraveling.

It was clear to Autumn that even in death, Samantha Monroe was still the most powerful person in the room.

* * *

Later that evening, Autumn sat at the edge of Brooklyn's guest bed wrapped in a white robe, but her mind stayed trapped in black. The air smelled like lavender and disappointment. Her Italian leather planner lay open across her lap, pages filled with past flights, board meetings, brand partnerships, brunch panels, fake smiles, and now...an obsolete identity.

Every square was color-coded perfection, carefully maintained like an altar to productivity. But today, it felt like an obituary to someone she no longer was.

She flipped to an old page: *Coffee w/ Samantha – 8:30 am – Violet Rose Café*

The ink curled like a question mark. Autumn's throat tightened. That morning was etched into her memory like marble. Samantha, wrapped in vintage Gucci and weaponized charisma, had slid a vision across the table for a woman-led empire that would be socially conscious, spiritually branded, and infinitely profitable. But underneath all that glitter and girlboss lingo was...grooming.

"How did I not see it?" Autumn whispered.

From the bathroom, Brooklyn called out between toothbrush swipes, "Because we were taught to trust the people who clapped the loudest."

Autumn gave a brittle laugh. "I gave her so much power."

"No, you gave her access." Brooklyn stepped into the room in a gold silk bonnet, her edges flawless. "Power's what she took after she earned your trust."

Autumn glanced back at the planner. Next to the coffee date was a note in Samantha's handwriting written in the margins: *Don't forget, Brees: Perception is price.*

It used to sound like a strategy. Now it reads like a threat.

"She had folders on everyone," Autumn muttered. "Clients. Staff. Me. Hazel. Even Jerald. She knew all our leverage."

"And nobody knew hers," Brooklyn said. "That's the real game."

Autumn nodded slowly. "She made herself untouchable. But now I think...maybe she was scared all along."

Brooklyn grew quiet. "Now she's gone and you're left holding what she didn't have the courage to tell."

The silence settled heavily between them. Brooklyn glanced down at the buzzing phone in her hand.

"Serenity just texted. She wants to meet you. Said she has something Sam left behind."

Autumn's body tensed.

"What is it?" she asked.

Brooklyn shrugged.

"Didn't say. Just that it's time."

Autumn looked back at her planner one last time, then shut it.

"Set it up."

* * *

The café Serenity chose had no menu and no ego, just reclaimed wood, local beans, and the vibe of intentional minimalism. Autumn showed up draped in black like a grieving celebrity, oversized shades, black turtleneck, all the performance of composure.

Serenity, true to form, wore white. Always white.

Like peace was her protest.

"You can drop the armor," Serenity said before Autumn even sat down.

Autumn blinked. "Excuse me?"

"The smile. The posture. That 'I'm fine' energy," Serenity replied gently. "You don't have to perform for me."

Autumn sat down slowly. "How do you always see through people?"

"Because I used to *be* people," Serenity said with a faint smile. "I know what pain looks like when it's stitched into couture."

They ordered coffee. Autumn never drank hers.

After a moment, Serenity reached into her canvas bag and pulled out a small leather-bound journal. Gold initials shimmered in the sunlight. **S.M.**

"She left this with me three weeks before she died," Serenity said quietly. "Told me to give it to you when you were ready."

Autumn stared at it like it might detonate.

"She said it held truth...and pain...and legacy," Serenity added. "But more than that, she said it held her confession."

Autumn's voice cracked. "Why now?"

"Because I saw something in you yesterday," Serenity said. "Something I hadn't seen before."

"What?"

"Surrender," she whispered. "Not survival. Not strength. Surrender."

Autumn looked down. Her tears came like apologies.

"I loved her," she said. "Even when I didn't trust her."

Serenity nodded.

"You still do. That's what makes this hard."

Autumn reached for the journal. It was heavier than it looked.

Back in Brooklyn's guest room, Autumn stared at the journal on her lap. Her phone buzzed. It was a text from Serenity: *Healing is violent before it's sacred. Read slowly.*

Autumn took a breath and flipped to the first page.

*"Brees, if you're reading this, I'm probably gone. And if I'm gone, it means the secrets caught up to me."*

She slammed it shut. She closed her eyes and tried to slow her breathing.

In that moment, it wasn't grief or sadness that overtook her. It was fear. The kind that comes when you realize you didn't just lose a mentor, and you're about to find out who they *really* were.

# PART II

## THE DETOX

# Therapy Is a Mirror

The scent of sandalwood clung to the room like a memory. Sunlight spilled across shelves filled with worn devotionals, leather-bound journals, and black-and-white photos of ancestors who seemed to know all your secrets. Autumn sat on the velvet couch, arms folded across her chest like armor, her eyes still swollen from crying in the car. She scanned the space for safety, or maybe just something familiar.

"I know I can't officially be your therapist," Serenity said, her voice soft but anchored. "Not with our history. Not with how close we all were...with Sam."

Autumn nodded. "I know. I just didn't know who else to call."

"I'm here," Serenity said. "As a sister in spirit. I'll help guide you. But I'll also connect you with someone who can walk with you professionally."

Autumn's shoulders sank slightly. She hadn't come for a diagnosis. She came for discernment. Accountability. Someone who knew her wounds by name but still believed in her healing.

"We'll walk this together," Serenity continued. "But I won't blur your process just to soothe you. You don't need comfort. You need clarity."

"I didn't come for therapy," Autumn whispered. "I just didn't want to sit in silence by myself."

"I know," Serenity said gently. "But because we've shared grief and faith and Samantha, there are lines I won't cross. Therapy is sacred, and you deserve someone who doesn't already know your ghosts."

Autumn gave a small, wry smile.

"So, what does that make this?"

"This," Serenity said, gesturing between them, "is sacred space. Spiritual companionship. Two women who've seen too much to pretend and survived too much to stay silent."

Autumn's voice cracked. "You saw it, didn't you? The shift in Sam...before everything fell apart?"

"I did," Serenity admitted. "But I was too wrapped in hope. Too busy trying to keep the peace between you two."

Autumn leaned back against the couch. Her words came out like a confession.

"I kept wondering if everyone saw it and just didn't say anything."

"I saw fragments, but guilt and hindsight love to lie, and I won't let them lead your healing."

A beat of silence stretched between them. Holy. Weighty.

"I'm not here to fix you," Serenity said. "But I can hold space while you rise. I'll help you find someone trained, someone who can tend to betrayal trauma without already knowing your highlight reel."

Autumn nodded, her eyes glistening. "Thank you for being honest...and kind."

Serenity handed her a folded slip of paper. "This is a therapist I trust. Black woman. No ties to the circle. She'll help you find your way back to yourself."

Autumn clutched it like scripture.

"Can we still pray together?" she asked.

"Always," Serenity said, reaching for her hands. "That's a great place to start."

Later that afternoon, Autumn sat stiffly in the passenger seat of Serenity's forest-green Tesla, clutching a lukewarm bottle of kombucha. The silence between them was sacred, the kind of stillness that follows funerals or precedes confession.

"I almost didn't come today," Autumn murmured.

Serenity nodded, eyes on the road. "That's how I knew you needed to."

They pulled up to a small brick bungalow draped in lavender and hydrangea. A wooden sign on the porch read: *Healing Happens Here.*

Inside, the air was thick with the scents of eucalyptus, lemon balm, and frankincense. No ticking clocks. No bright lights. Just space. Breath. Presence.

Autumn settled into a velvet green chair near a bay window. Across from her, books on trauma and Black womanhood lined the shelves. A framed Rumi quote on the wall caught her eye: *"The wound is where the Light enters you."*

Serenity reentered barefoot, carrying a tray with tea, lemon, honey, tissues, and a soft leather journal embossed with Autumn's name in gold foil.

She set it down gently.

"You've been carrying yourself like luggage, and it's time to unpack."

Autumn exhaled. "I don't even know where to start."

"Start with what you feel," Serenity said. "Not what you've built. Not what you've lost. Just what you feel."

"I feel tired," Autumn said, voice thin. "Angry. Embarrassed. Like I'm grieving someone who's still breathing. But that someone is...me."

Serenity nodded. "That's a funeral worth attending."

Autumn blinked back tears. "I gave everything to the image. I performed worthiness. I polished the pain. Now I'm broke, financially, yes, but soul-broke, too." She paused. "I don't even know who I am without the brand. Without Sam."

Serenity leaned in. "Do you want to find out?"

Autumn nodded.

Serenity rose and returned with an antique mirror, gold-trimmed, cracked in one corner.

"Look, but don't flinch."

Autumn stared. At first, she only saw exhaustion through the bags under her eyes and the sadness in her posture. But beneath the fatigue, there was a flicker. A breath. A woman not lost, just buried.

"I don't recognize her," she whispered.

"She's not gone," Serenity said. "She's under the hustle. Under betrayal. Under someone else's spotlight. But she's still here. And she's tired of apologizing for existing."

Autumn wiped her face.

"I miss her."

"Then let's reintroduce you."

A long breath passed between them.

"Before we go any deeper, tell me about Samantha Monroe. I was at her funeral, so I know some of your thoughts, but I never really understood your full history with her."

Autumn hesitated.

"Sam was...everything. My mentor. My storm. My lesson. She gave me my first shot. Made me feel chosen. But it wasn't love. It was control. A cage disguised as opportunity."

"So, you believe she used you?" Serenity asked, gently but clearly.

"She did. She forged my name on documents. Signed deals without me. Said it was for the brand." Autumn looked away. "I let her. I wanted to believe it was all for us."

"Did you love her?"

"I don't know," Autumn whispered. "I think I loved who I thought she was. Or who I became around her."

Serenity let that settle. "Sometimes we're trauma-bonded, not soul-connected. When someone teaches you survival instead of healing, you start to confuse pain with intimacy."

Autumn doubled over, sobbing, not politely, not carefully. She wept in the way that erases years of pretending.

Serenity didn't interrupt. She witnessed it because this was the real work. Not the rebrand. Not the retreat. Not the podcast. This was deliverance.

When the wave passed, Serenity reached for the journal.

"This is where you begin," she said softly. "Not with your résumé or your receipts but with your remembrance."

Autumn took it, holding it to her chest as if it were scripture.

Outside, the clouds began to break.

Inside?

So did she.

* * *

The rooftop patio was a garden in the sky, orchids draped around champagne flutes, soft gospel jazz floating on the breeze, and women cloaked in elegance that whispered wealth and walked like worship. Every detail glimmered with intention: gold-inked name cards, a signature mocktail called *The Revival* at each place setting, and the unmistakable imprint of Samantha Monroe.

Autumn stood near the glass railing, Charlotte's skyline rising before her, overdressed and underprepared. The invitation had come at the last minute, like most things with Sam. A text that sounded more like a command than a request: *Come ready to shine. This one's intimate. My circle only.*

Behind her, laughter rose like a Sunday crescendo. Samantha floated through the space with high-gloss grace, hugging, air-kissing, and dazzling. She moved like a woman who had already survived the fire and now walked through the smoke untouched.

"Autumn," Sam called, her voice a soft beckon wrapped in authority. "Come meet someone you didn't know you needed."

Autumn adjusted her heels, smoothed her skirt, and crossed the tiled patio.

Samantha led her to a small round table tucked beneath an ivy trellis. Seated there, sipping hibiscus tea and crowned in locs that shimmered like sunlit copper, was a woman who radiated peace and purpose.

"Serenity Sanders," Sam said with matchmaking pride, "is a licensed therapist, preacher's daughter, and stays quiet enough to hear God before He actually speaks."

Serenity stood—graceful, grounded, present. Her eyes didn't scan Autumn's outfit or résumé. They looked *into* her, like she'd already seen her weeping on the floor, and still chose to call her sister.

Autumn blinked, taken off guard. "I've heard of your healing circles. You host them, right?"

Serenity smiled. "I hold space. The healing is God's."

Autumn's corporate confidence didn't quite know what to do with Serenity's kind of softness.

Samantha beamed, arms folded like a proud matriarch. "You two are cut from the same cloth. Different patterns, but same divine thread. Just wait. You'll see." With that, she winked and left them to find their own way.

They sat together for nearly an hour, not discussing trauma, but unearthing joy. They spoke of poetry, Black girlhood, and being too sensitive in boardrooms and too ambitious in churches. They exchanged numbers, but more than that, they exchanged *energy*.

Autumn didn't know it five years ago, but she'd need Serenity one day, not just as a therapist, but as a *witness* to the unraveling of everything Samantha once claimed to build.

* * *

It was supposed to be a prayer meeting.

Serenity Sanders stepped into Samantha Monroe's office, pausing at the threshold. The space still smelled of lavender polish and fresh contracts. Gold light poured through floor-to-ceiling windows, illuminating every curated surface. On the desk sat a gold-plated pen that looked too heavy to tell the truth.

Sam's assistant had apologized, saying she was running behind. But Serenity already sensed it. This wasn't prayer. This was performance.

Three women sat in the corner, dressed like investment pitches. One clutched a media deck stamped with Sam's embossed logo. Another whispered about brand expansion. There were no Bibles. No reverence. Just the hum of ambition dressed up as divine calling. The Spirit had already left the room.

Serenity walked toward the far wall where a photo hung of Sam and Autumn, arms linked, with mentees at a wellness retreat. Everyone had their eyes closed, heads tilted to the sun like sunflowers in bloom.

But the woman in the center, poised in a white jumpsuit, smiling wide, looked different now. Still beautiful and bold, but no longer soft. No longer still.

Just then, the door opened.

Samantha swept in like a storm wearing silk. She was radiant, curated, and overly composed.

"Ladies!" she sang, hands lifted in faux humility. "Thank you for being patient. The vision is expanding faster than expected." Her voice sparkled, but her spirit cracked at the seams.

She hugged Serenity last. It was a performative squeeze wrapped in tension. In her eyes, Serenity saw it. Not guilt. Not shame. Just...absence.

They sat. Sam led a prayer that was technically correct and scripturally sound, but it didn't rise like a knowing flame. It dropped to the floor like strategy.

After the other women left, Serenity lingered.

"You okay?" she asked, her voice gentle but grounded.

Sam turned to the window, sipping from a crystal tumbler.

"Why wouldn't I be? We're building a legacy and global impact. You should see what's next."

Serenity didn't smile. "That's not what I asked."

Sam's jaw tensed. "I'm fine, just tired. You know how leadership gets."

Serenity's gaze didn't waver. "No," she said softly. "I know how *discernment* gets, and something's not right."

The pause between them was spiritual tension, thick with history.

Sam turned. Her tone sharpened. "I hope you're not judging me."

"I'm interceding," Serenity replied. "But I can't cover what you keep cloaked."

Sam's eyes narrowed, and that's when Serenity *saw it*. Not just ambition and fatigue, but compromise. Small. Layered. Sharp like glass under bare feet.

Serenity stood, gathering her coat.

"You're not beyond grace, Sam. But you *are* beyond me now. If you ever want me to pray, I will. But I can't walk beside you through something built on illusion."

She left without slamming the door because sometimes, exits don't need noise. Just clarity.

# The Hustle & The Haunting

The phone rang just as Autumn kicked off her heels and reached for her journal. She ignored it. Therapy with Serenity had left her raw, like someone had taken a wire brush to the walls of her soul. All she wanted was silence. Maybe to write something poetic about surrender, healing, and not falling apart in the middle of the grocery store again.

The phone rang again. It was Brooklyn. She sighed and answered.

"Hey, I just—"

"She's gone, Autumn."

Brooklyn's voice was quiet. Shaky. Not her usual fire.

Autumn blinked. "What? Who's gone? What happened?"

"Granny. She passed this morning. Mama just called me. She'd been declining fast but..." Brooklyn's voice cracked. "I thought we had more time."

Autumn sat down, barefoot on a cold tile. The world tilted.

"No, no, no, no. I was supposed to visit her this weekend. I have her birthday gift still wrapped on my counter."

"I know. Me too."

A pause stretched between them. Grief entered the room and sat down like it owned the place.

"Was she in pain?" Autumn asked.

"They said she went in her sleep."

Autumn exhaled shakily. "Peaceful, I guess."

"That woman was never peaceful a day in her life," Autumn muttered, bitter laughter breaking through the ache.

Brooklyn chuckled through her tears.

"You're right. She probably argued with God on the way up."

"She probably corrected Him."

Then quiet again.

"You okay?" Brooklyn asked gently.

Autumn stared at the blank journal page in front of her.

"No," she whispered. For once, she didn't feel the need to pretend otherwise.

That evening, Serenity came over with lemon balm tea and eyes full of concern.

"She mattered to you," she said gently, after Autumn explained through tears. "Even with the wounds. Especially with the wounds."

"She was the last woman in our bloodline who remembered the stories," Autumn whispered. "The ones about the land. The babies we never talked about. What it costs to be Black and brilliant and a woman in this world…"

Serenity nodded. "So, let's remember her, Autumn. Not just what hurt, but what helped. Let's talk about what grief wants to do to you."

"What does grief want to do?" Autumn asked, her voice small.

"Crush your identity," Serenity said. "But if you name it, it becomes a river instead of a dam. You get to decide what flows forward."

Autumn wiped her face. "I just didn't want to lose her before she saw me whole again."

"She saw you. Even in the mess. She saw what you were becoming."

"I hope she sees me now."

"She does." Serenity placed the mug in her hands. "And she's cheering louder than anyone."

* * *

Autumn was ten, curled on the edge of her grandmother's bed. Colorful fabric scraps and sharp pins took up the remainder of the space.

"Baby girl," Granny said, holding up a vibrant piece of Ankara print, "don't you ever throw away what tried to break you. Stitch it."

"But it's ripped," Autumn frowned.

"Everything ripped has a story," Granny replied, steady hands at work. "A strong woman knows how to patch the pain with purpose."

She reached for a square of fabric with tiny roses embroidered in the corner.

"This was your great aunt Etta's apron," she said softly. "She cooked Sunday dinners with her whole soul, even after her husband left. Fed a whole block full of babies who never knew what they were missing."

Autumn picked up a strip of denim. "What about this one?"

Granny chuckled. "That? That's from your mama's old jacket. She wore it in college, thought she was Angela Davis and Janet Jackson rolled into one."

Autumn giggled. "She did have the hair."

Granny smiled.

"This quilt ain't just for warmth, baby. It's a legacy. And one day, you gon' make your own. Sew it with whatever God gives you."

* * *

Autumn jolted awake, breath ragged, drenched in sweat. Brooklyn stood in the doorway, holding peppermint water and a towel. Her hoodie hung off one shoulder, mascara smudged like grief that refused to be washed away.

"You screamed her name," she said quietly. "Three times."

Autumn wiped her face, peppermint cooling her skin but not the fire in her chest.

"I think she's still here."

Brooklyn sat beside her, shoulder to shoulder.

"She is," she whispered.

The rain tapped softly against the sunroom windows.

Autumn sat cross-legged on the floor, surrounded by damp boxes and the scent of mildew. Her scarf was loose. Her socks mismatched. She hadn't meant to open the box labeled SAM. But grief doesn't ask permission. It picks locks.

Right on top sat Samantha's burnt-orange leather journal. Autumn froze, then opened it. The first entry was five years old.

*Power is a perfume. It doesn't matter how much you have, it's how you wear it. But Lord help me… this scent is starting to choke me.*

Autumn's hands trembled as she turned the page.

*They call me a mogul, but some days I feel like a magician. I've finessed contracts, dodged audits, and repackaged the truth so many times, I barely recognize it anymore. I wonder if Breezy will ever know how deep this rabbit hole goes.*

*Breezy.* Only Granny and Sam had called her that. She flipped again.

*I never meant to hurt her. But she believed in me too much. Trusted too quickly. That's what made it so easy.*

Autumn dropped the journal as if it burned. *Easy?* It had been *easy* to hurt her. She doubled over, grief morphing into rage. But then, another page slipped loose.

*She's the daughter I never had. God gave her to me in the form I could never carry.*

A tear slid down her cheek.

"You always knew how to make lies sound holy," she whispered.

There was a soft knock on the door. Then Brooklyn peeked into the sunroom.

"You good?"

Autumn held up the journal. "I opened it."

Brooklyn sat beside her.

"She played me, and I let her."

"You loved her."

"I did. Like a sister. Now I don't know what was real."

"That's the worst kind of betrayal," Brooklyn said. "The kind that wears your favorite perfume and knows your PIN."

Autumn half-laughed through her tears.

"She made me the face of one of the deals. I didn't know until the lawsuit hit. By then, she was gone."

Brooklyn's jaw clenched. "Is that why you left?"

"I couldn't show my face. I was guilty by proximity."

Brooklyn rubbed her shoulder. "Yet, here you are. Still breathing."

Autumn exhaled. "Still broken."

The rain tapped like baptism. Brooklyn finally asked what they both feared.

"You think someone killed her because of this?"

Autumn swallowed hard. "I don't know. But that journal? It doesn't sound like someone who was planning to live much longer."

She opened it and showed Brooklyn an entry.

*Legacy is a liar when it's built on borrowed truth. I taught her how to sell dreams, but I never told her what they cost. If anything happens to me, tell Breezy I'm sorry I didn't stop when I should have. I should've walked away. But greed was louder than guilt.*

Brooklyn went pale. Autumn clutched the journal.

"God, what am I supposed to do with this?"

Then, in the stillness only truth can bring, she heard it, not with ears, but in spirit.

*Tell the truth. Start with Me.*

* * *

Just four years earlier, Sam had stood barefoot on her back porch, sipping ginger tea from a chipped mug. Conflicting thoughts plagued her mind as she took in her surroundings. Behind her, a familiar creak came from the screen door.

"Ma," said Caleb. He stepped outside, quiet, heavy, unreadable. "Have you ever thought about how legacy skips people?" he asked.

"I think legacy waits on obedience," Sam said slowly. "But sometimes people delay it with bitterness."

"You gave Autumn everything," Caleb murmured. "She ain't blood, but you gave her the keys."

"She was my assignment," Samantha said. "Just like you were... once."

"Assignments get finished. Family stays."

The wind stirred. The robe lifted at the edge. Secrets shifted.

"Are you threatening me, Caleb?" she asked.

He smiled with everything but warmth and sincerity, before turning and walking back inside.

Samantha stood in silence long after he'd left, whispering to the sky.

"Cover him, Lord. Before I become his undoing."

# CHAPTER SIX

# Paperwork & Pain Points

The first time Autumn met Detective Marcus King, she was seated under fluorescent lights in a government building that smelled like old coffee and heavy truths. She hadn't expected the man across from her to be so...grounded.

He wore a black blazer, no tie. His beard was trimmed but not too clean. His eyes looked like they'd seen both war and worship.

He flipped through his notes while seated across from her at the sterile metal table. Then looked up at her directly. His dark eyes were steady, probing.

Autumn clenched her fists in her lap, fingers trembling beneath the weight of grief and suspicion.

"Ms. James," he began, voice low and firm, "I know this is hard. But I need you to tell me about Samantha Monroe. About your relationship with her and Caleb."

Autumn swallowed. Her mind tumbled through memories like glass in a dryer.

"Samantha was...complicated. A mentor, yes, but more than that. She saw something in me I didn't even know was there. Caleb was always on the edge. Brilliant but unstable."

Marcus leaned in slightly.

"If there's anything you haven't told me, anything at all, now's the time. I'm not here to judge. I'm here to find the truth. Maybe help you find some peace."

Her eyes lifted, searching for judgment. She found only a strange kindness.

"Peace feels like a lifetime away," she said softly.

Marcus offered a faint smile. "Maybe we start by being honest with each other."

A fragile thread stretched between them. For the first time since her world tilted, Autumn felt something close to safe.

"You were more than a business partner," Marcus said. His voice was warm now, almost teasing. "What would you say you were to her?"

Autumn blinked. "Complicated."

Marcus smiled. "That's the best kind of truth."

She noticed the corner of a worn brown Bible sticking out of his satchel. She paused.

"Have you ever met Sam before?" she asked him.

He hesitated, just a beat too long. "Yeah. Back when I was with CMPD. Had to investigate a few of her ventures."

"And?"

"She was ten steps ahead of everybody. Sharp. Dangerous. Not someone I'd go into business with, no offense."

Autumn gave a dry laugh. "None taken."

But something flickered in his eyes. A secret behind his clean-cut edges. The kind of flicker that hid behind church boys who carried both Scripture and scars.

* * *

Later that week, Autumn stood outside Hazel Youngblood's law office like it was a confession booth. The building was all glass and steel, clean lines, hard truths.

But her heart? That was messy. Raw. Barely stitched together.

Hazel didn't waste time. "Let's talk about legacy and lawsuits."

The office was sun-drenched and layered with law books and wall affirmations like, "Black women don't break, we pivot."

Hazel wore a cranberry pantsuit and her signature stare: no nonsense, no wiggle room.

"You want an empire?" she asked. "Then let's build one that can't be burned down by betrayal." She tapped a thick folder on her desk.

"I knew Samantha for years," Hazel said. "She was brilliant and dangerous. I was her lawyer. I saw both sides. The visionary and the woman cutting corners when it suited her."

"She made loyalty feel like gospel," Hazel added. "It's why women like you never questioned her."

Autumn sat forward, voice cracking. "Why didn't anyone stop her?"

Hazel shrugged. "Because respect and fear look similar in the dark. But now? I'm not working for her. I'm here for *you*."

Hazel opened the folder. Contracts from the Brees Branded venture lay inside like funeral programs.

"This notary seal? Fake." She tapped it. "This signature? Slanted wrong. That's not your handwriting."

Autumn stared at the page.

"Wait...so I didn't sign this?"

"No," Hazel said. "Samantha used your name, your brand, and your face, but she never gave you ownership. She dressed you up to make the deal look clean."

Autumn's jaw dropped. "She said I was protected."

Hazel didn't flinch. "No, you were *positioned*."

Tears burned in Autumn's eyes. "We had a bond."

Hazel corrected her gently.

"*You* had a bond. She had a blueprint."

Autumn leaned back in her chair, blinking against the sting. Her signature, copied. Her name, misused. Her purpose, blurred.

Hazel laid out another sheet. "She funneled money through your name. If we don't clean this up, the IRS will come for you."

Autumn's voice shook. "Wait, what? Funneled money? But she said she loved me. That we were building something powerful together."

Hazel's expression didn't soften. "She built it on your back."

Autumn stood, anger flaring like sudden heat.

"I want to press charges."

Hazel raised a brow, then smiled faintly. "Good. But first, we file *your* paperwork. Real paperwork. This time, God gets a say."

They spent the next four hours rebuilding from ash. New LLCs. Real contracts. Protection clauses. Ownership agreements with Autumn's name on the line.

When Autumn finally left, she held a binder full of beginnings. But the real wound followed her out the door. She sat in her car and pressed play on the last voicemail Sam ever left.

"Breezy, I made you cold so the world wouldn't burn you.

But baby girl, it's time to thaw."

Autumn closed her eyes. *You didn't protect me, you played me. But I'm done playing myself.*

She exhaled and started the engine, still seated in the car outside Hazel's office. The betrayal sat heavy. But so did clarity. This wasn't the end. This was the start.

She stared out the window and thought, *This time, I will have legitimate contracts, know the terms, and always sign my own name.*

Autumn had shown up late to the women's business brunch. She stumbled in with too many business cards and not enough confidence.

Her startup? Still mostly a dream on Google Docs. The women around her were glossy, radiant with funding, and had impressive Instagram captions. She was frayed denim wrapped in ambition.

She sat near the back, scanning her folder.

Then came a voice.

"Don't shrink. It's bad for business."

She looked up. Samantha Monroe stood in a cream pantsuit and red lipstick like a gospel song dipped in thunder.

"I'm Sam," she said, sliding into the seat beside her. "I used to be that woman, shrinking to fit into rooms. Now I build the rooms."

Autumn smiled nervously. "I'm Autumn. Mostly here for the croissants."

Sam chuckled. "That's the best reason I've heard all day."

They ignored the keynote speaker, whispering like choir girls in the back pew. Sam asked about her business idea and actually listened. She pulled a napkin from her bag and scribbled something down.

"You've got vision, Breezy," she said. "And if you trust me, I'll help you build a bridge from passion to profit."

"Did you just nickname me?"

"Absolutely. Everybody needs a name that reminds them they're not their past or their paycheck. Breezy suits you. You're wind. Unstoppable. When you move, things shift."

Autumn laughed. But something in her shifted. She felt seen.

They stayed long after the room emptied, talking about pitch decks, pressure, and how no one warned Black girls that brilliance could be lonely.

"You remind me of myself at twenty-seven," Sam said. "But softer. That's your power. Don't let the world harden it."

That had been six years ago, and it was one piece of advice Autumn could no longer follow.

* * *

Sam was no stranger to law enforcement. Three years ago, she'd sat under a dryer at Curly Crown, cucumber water in hand, flawless in a cream jumpsuit and curls bouncing like royalty. Autumn sat in the next chair, head tilted back as Jada detangled gently. Then Tamia stormed in.

"Samantha Monroe," she spat. "World-class entrepreneur, low-class whore."

The salon froze.

Camille glanced up, murder in her eyes. "Want me to handle this?"

Sam didn't blink. "Maybe."

Tamia pointed, hands shaking.

"You slept with my husband. You scammed our business. You had a child."

Sam stood. Clicked her heels like punctuation.

"You want attention? Let's give you some. Your man liked heels. You should try them."

Tamia screamed, "He'd never choose you!"

Sam snapped, "Sweetheart, he *married* me."

Silence.

"But the second you mentioned my son? You crossed a line."

Camille grabbed Tamia by the arm and escorted her out like yesterday's weave.

Later that day, Detective Marcus King arrived at Samantha's office.

"Ms. Monroe," he said, badge gleaming. "There's a warrant out for your cousin."

Sam crossed her legs. "CMPD delivers misdemeanor warrants now?"

Marcus glanced around. "I was also looking for the girl with the ponytail and trauma eyes."

Sam smirked. "Autumn James. Yeah, that one's stitched together with ambition and duct tape."

"She deserves to be loved like something sacred," Marcus said softly.

Sam tilted her head. "Then love her slowly. Don't fix her. Just be there when the bandage comes off."

# PART III

## THE AWAKENING

# CHAPTER SEVEN

# Broke Is a Season, Not a Sentence

Autumn sat in Serenity's office, her voice low and scraped raw. "I signed everything. No lawyer. Just faith."

Serenity leaned forward, her gaze unwavering.

"Let's name that honestly, Autumn. That wasn't faith. That was emotional loyalty. That was an unhealed need disguised as trust."

Autumn blinked quickly, staring past the floor.

"She moved all the money...in my name. Every investor, every 'deal'...she disappeared before the feds even knocked." Her throat tightened. "I lost everything. My business. My reputation. My savings. I was a hashtag. *#BreesBankrupt.*"

Serenity handed her a tissue without fanfare.

"Yet, you're still here. That's not failure, Autumn. That's resurrection."

"But I'm angry," Autumn whispered. "Angry at myself for needing her and for wanting to be seen so badly. I ignored every warning."

"That's grief, baby," Serenity said gently. "It'll trick your mirror. Make you see potential where there's manipulation. But we'll heal that girl, one mirror at a time."

Later that week, Autumn sat at her laptop. Her account balances felt like cruel poetry:

| | |
|---|---|
| **Checking:** | $17.32 |
| **Savings:** | $0.00 |
| **Credit Cards:** | Declined |
| **Faith:** | Disappearing |

She whispered into the stillness, voice cracking:

"God, why did you call me out here to fail?"

She hadn't realized she'd said it aloud until Brooklyn walked in, arms full of groceries and an expression that said she already knew.

"Need anything else?"

"A new life," Autumn muttered.

Brooklyn handed her a green smoothie.

"This one comes with fiber and faith."

They sat in silence until Brooklyn nudged her gently.

"Come to church with me tomorrow."

The next morning, Grace Community Church smelled of frankincense and restoration. As they entered, Autumn's heels clicked against the worn hardwood floors. Light poured through stained glass like grace broken into color.

Brooklyn leaned over and whispered., "This is where I laid down my shame."

The sermon rose and fell around them. The pastor preached about seasons. The kind that breaks you, strips you, teaches you how to bloom from bone.

Autumn closed her eyes. She didn't cry. Not yet. But something inside her cracked open.

After service, Brooklyn led her to a circle of women near the altar. It was full of entrepreneurs, survivors, misfits, and mothers, all tethered by grit and grace. Serenity was there. So was Hazel, still sharp, but softer now.

Autumn sat slowly. When her turn came, she surprised herself.

"I'm broke," she said.

No one flinched.

"Not just financially. But soul broke. Spirit broke. I've been hustling for so long, I forgot how to be human."

Brooklyn squeezed her hand. "Broke is a season. Not a sentence."

Serenity nodded. "It's where surrender begins."

Hazel added, eyes steady, "And from surrender, we build. But with boundaries this time."

Autumn didn't cry. She *breathed,* and that felt like healing.

That afternoon, they attended Serenity's healing brunch. Sunlight filtered through fig trees as laughter rippled around them like water.

Detective Marcus King was there. Quiet. Observing.

He watched Autumn hand out granola bars, smile gently at elders, and laugh with young girls like they were her little sisters. When their eyes met across the courtyard, something passed between them.

He approached slowly.

"Didn't expect to see you here," Autumn said, stepping to the side.

"I wanted to see this for myself," Marcus replied, voice low. "You're doing something real here."

She looked down, then up again.

"It's been the only place I've felt whole lately."

"You're stronger than you think."

Later, by the punch bowl, he found her again.

"You spoke life today," he said.

"I wasn't trying to," Autumn replied, voice fragile.

Marcus looked at her, his voice softer than she expected.

"My mama used to say healing is holy work. And you, you've got holy hands. Even if they're trembling."

Autumn's eyes welled. She looked away.

"No one's ever said that to me."

"I see you," he said quietly.

She believed him.

That week, Autumn met Nadine Love, a local entrepreneur who had filed for bankruptcy twice before launching a million-dollar candle business from her stove.

They sat on Nadine's porch, sipping peppermint tea from mismatched mugs.

"Being broke is humbling," Nadine said. "But it's holy. You meet God when He's your only investor."

"What about being scared?"

"That's just faith in reverse. Flip it forward."

Before she left, Nadine handed Autumn a candle labeled **Don't Quit on Day 3.**

That night, she lit it and let the scent of cedar and lemon balm fill her room. The candle flickered low. Wax pooled gently in its center like a prayer answered slowly. Autumn traced the label with her finger. She closed her eyes, exhaled softly, and whispered into the quiet.

"Broke is a season. But I am still becoming."

At that moment, she believed it.

As she breathed and dreamt.

In her dream, Autumn stood in a velvet-lit room. Candlelight flickered. The scent of jasmine and something sacred hung in the air. Then, he appeared. Detective Marcus King stepped from the shadows. Calm. Steady. Safe.

"You feel like home," she whispered.

He walked toward her. No rush. No performance. Just presence.

His kiss was soft. Reverent. Like a man who knew pain and wanted to honor hers.

When he held her, she wept, not because she was weak, but because she didn't have to be strong.

* * *

It was almost midnight when Autumn called her mother. Her voice trembled through the line.

"Mama? I...I need you."

Her mother's voice was quiet. Flat.

"I'm tired, Autumn. I can't always be your rock."

The line crackled with silence.

"I didn't mean to—"

"You always mean well, baby. But I've got my own load. Goodnight."

The call ended. Autumn sat in the dark, feeling more alone than ever. But in her gut, she also understood. Her mother was human. Not a savior. And maybe, just maybe, it was time to become her own.

# CHAPTER EIGHT

# Broken Deals, Broken Dreams

Autumn's phone buzzed on the kitchen counter. CALEB MONROE filled the screen. She froze. Her thumb hovered over the screen. For a moment, she hoped, maybe this would be the call where they'd share memories. Where grief softened enough to make space for healing.

She answered.

"Caleb, hey. I didn't think I'd hear from you. I...I miss her too."

A long silence.

Then his voice, lower than she remembered, clipped and cold.

"You ever wonder why she picked you?"

Autumn blinked. "What are you talking about?"

"You had everything. A last name. Parents. Money. Options. Still, she gave you everything."

Her stomach tightened. "She loved you, Caleb. You were her family."

Another pause.

"Then why didn't she leave it to me?"

The line clicked. Gone.

Autumn stared at the screen, jaw trembling. Her grief curdled into something harder. Not just sorrow, but suspicion. Then grief's bitter twin, betrayal.

* * *

It started with a DM.

*Tiana West.*

Verified. Massive platform. Polished influencer in pearls and scripture. She'd called Autumn's voice "anointed," her story "an activation for a generation."

Autumn had been flattered. Hungry for purpose. Still aching for redemption.

The offer? A summit for powerhouse women of faith.

The contract? Quick, but clean.

The pitch? Spirit-led collaboration.

The deposit? Processing.

Then...nothing. One week. Then two. No reply. No wire. Just ghosts. Until Brooklyn crashed through the door one morning, her phone in hand.

"Sit down," she said. "Now."

Autumn's eyes tracked the screen as Tiana's promo reel played. She watched *her* idea, *her* words, and even the graphic she'd mocked up on Canva flash across the screen, but nowhere was her name.

"She stole everything," Autumn said just above a whisper.

"Blocked you, too," Brooklyn added. "Whole team."

Autumn dropped onto the couch, air knocked clean from her lungs.

"I'm done. I'm not built for this."

An hour later, Hazel arrived like a holy hurricane. Burgundy blazer, blunt bob, and a Bible and binder under one arm.

"Let me see the contract," she said, already flipping through the pages.

Two pages in, she snorted.

"This fool left the wrong name in the footer. Sloppy copy and paste from an old NDA. Rookie mistake."

She sat on her couch, shoulders tense, heart raw.

"I ignored every red flag," Autumn said to no one in particular. "She didn't just mentor me. She crafted me."

Brooklyn sat beside her, voice firm.

"It's time to unlearn that gospel."

"What gospel?"

"That loyalty means silence. That discernment is disrespectful. That being chosen means you owe them everything—your voice, your body, your brand."

Autumn buried her face in her hands. "I don't want to be strategic anymore. I want to be *spirit-led.*"

Brooklyn touched her back. "Then stop performing. Start praying."

Autumn blinked. "So, what do we do?"

Hazel smirked. "We fight with wisdom, not wrath. Spirit and statute."

Brooklyn nodded. "We got you."

Autumn nodded, but her gaze drifted. Backward. Back to how this all began.

* * *

Two years earlier, a Gulfstream G650 had shimmered on the tarmac like a divine chariot. Samantha Monroe descended in Chanel shades and a gold-threaded kaftan, arms wide as her influence.

"There she is!" Sam called. "The future of the brand!"

Cameras flashed and applause echoed.

"Sam, you don't have to hype me like that."

"But I *do*, Breezy," Sam whispered, linking their arms. "People follow what's affirmed. If I crown you, they'll believe in you, too."

Autumn smiled, flattered, and flinched beneath it.

Sam leaned close. Her voice was velvet-wrapped steel.

"Never second-guess confidence. Trust me, I've been playing this game longer than you've been drinking wine."

Later that night, Sam slid a crisp NDA across a marble table. There were no lawyers, just champagne and charm.

"Let me lead you," Sam whispered. "I'll make sure you're unforgettable."

Autumn smiled and signed. She never got a copy.

* * *

That evening, Autumn arrived home to find a letter waiting. It was handwritten with no return address.

The script was firm but unfamiliar, like healing with a limp. Her mother.

*I wasn't the mother you needed. But I'm trying to be the woman who sees you now. You deserved more and I hope someday, you'll let me try again.*

Autumn clutched it to her chest. Not forgiveness but a fragile bridge. She called Marcus and asked him to stop by.

The city's glow spilled in from the windows as Marcus sat beside her on the couch.

"Do you ever feel like you're carrying too much?" he asked, his voice soft.

Autumn nodded.

"Every day. But I've learned to put it down. Even if just for a moment."

"Why didn't you bring this to God before you signed?"

Autumn's voice cracked. "Because I wanted to win."

Marcus paused before asking, "And what did it cost you?"

Autumn didn't answer but she cried. Not because she was weak but because she was waking up.

He looked over at her, something unspoken swimming in his eyes.

"Faith's hardest when it's darkest."

Autumn's voice trembled but didn't break.

"But it's also the light we follow back."

Their hands brushed. Marcus took hers.

"Thank you," he whispered. "For reminding me hope still lives."

Autumn met his gaze, unguarded.

"I see you," he said.

For once, she didn't flinch from being seen.

* * *

Hazel walked into the next morning's meeting like a woman on assignment.

"We're going to clean this up. But you need new boundaries. Legal *and* spiritual."

Autumn nodded. Shame still stuck to her ribs.

Hazel looked straight at her.

"You weren't stupid. You were groomed. Trained to ignore your intuition in exchange for access. That's not your fault. But now?" She tapped the binder. "Now it's your responsibility."

Autumn's voice steadied.

"I'm done being used."

"Good," Hazel said. "Then let's protect what's yours."

That night, Autumn knelt beside her bed. Her voice barely a whisper.

"God, I'm broken but still here. Show me how to rise."

She didn't pray for revenge or applause. She prayed for clarity.

In her dream, a vast night sky stretched overhead, filled with stars that covered the abundance like scripture. Autumn stood on the edge of a bridge suspended over darkness. Marcus stood beside her. Silent. Steady.

"Take my hand," he said.

She did.

Beneath them, voices rose from the abyss. *Fraud! User! Failure!*

But Marcus never let go. When they reached the other side, he turned to her, his eyes a sanctuary.

"I see you," he said as he held her face in his hands.

Then he kissed her softly. Anchored. Certain. Not lust but rescue.

Autumn woke up with tears on her cheeks. But not for what she had lost. They were for who she was becoming. The storm hadn't ended, but she'd learned how to walk through it with her faith. With her fire. And this time, with no apologies.

She whispered into the morning light, "You didn't protect me, Sam. But I will protect myself now."

# CHAPTER NINE

# Sabbath & Surrender

There's a silence you only hear after surrender. It isn't empty. It hums with God.

Autumn stood barefoot on Brooklyn's balcony, wrapped in a white robe. The sunrise painted the Charlotte sky in lavender and honey, and for the first time in what felt like forever, her mind wasn't racing. It was the final day of her spiritual fast. No caffeine. No calls. No content. Just scripture, stillness, and the journal Samantha left behind, like both confession and curse.

For seven days, she had surrendered more than just food. She surrendered the performance, the pressure, and the obsession with being understood. Each morning, she cried. Not because she missed Samantha but because she finally missed herself.

Inside, the sunroom was hushed and holy. Autumn sat tucked beneath Serenity's gifted prayer shawl, Sam's journal heavy in her lap. She'd read it front to back, then again. Some parts felt like apologies. Others like strategies.

Today, one line refused to let her go.

"The girl's got a heart, but she's still green. I can mold her. Teach her how to play the room before the room plays her. She just needs someone to believe in her, and I'll be that. As long as she listens."

Her chest tightened from clarity. Did she feel rage? Regret?

No, it was grief finally given language.

Autumn's fingers pressed to her lips. *You didn't make me, Sam. You tested me. Eventually...I passed.*

She closed the journal slowly, not with bitterness, but with resolve. The manipulation didn't erase the moments of mentorship.

But it reframed the story.

Behind her, Brooklyn's playlist of Tasha Cobbs, Chandler Moore, and Kirk Franklin floated in like an anointing.

On the table inside, the thick folder Hazel had delivered sat ready and filled with incorporation paperwork, contracts, and a soul-centered intake process.

### Billionaire Broke Girls, LLC
*Wealth Begins Within.*

Hazel had raised an eyebrow when she saw the name.

"Are you sure about that? It's...loud."

"Exactly," Autumn replied. "So were we when we were hiding pain behind Prada and performance."

Hazel smirked. "You're finally getting it."

Autumn smiled at the memory, picked up her phone, and opened the camera. This time, no filter. No angles. Just her.

"Good morning," she said gently into the lens. "My name is Autumn Brees James and today, I'm launching something born from pain, prayer, and purpose."

She swallowed.

"This isn't just a business. This is a blueprint for every woman who lost herself trying to keep her income. For every girl who mastered performance and forgot her power. This one's for us."

She hit send.

That evening, Serenity arrived with white roses.

"You did it," she smiled.

"I don't know what 'it' is yet."

"Whatever *it* is," Serenity said, "it doesn't feel like hustle anymore. It feels like healing."

They sipped peppermint tea while gospel played in the background. Autumn's business plan sat beside Brooklyn's cookbook draft. It all felt sacred.

"I want to host a brunch," Autumn said. "Not at a ballroom but outside. Something like a table in the wilderness."

"With paper napkins and scriptures on them?" Serenity teased.

"Exactly."

"I like it. Divine marketing."

They heard a knock at the door. Brooklyn opened it to find Detective Marcus standing on the other side.

"Evening, ladies," he said with a grin.

"Marcus?" Autumn blinked. "What are you doing here?"

He held out a leather journal. "You left this in my car after Serenity's event."

Their hands brushed as she took it. Their eyes lingered.

"You okay?" he asked softly.

Autumn nodded. "Better than okay."

He stepped back, his smile crooked but steady.

"Good, because I think you're about to change lives."

She tilted her head. "Why do you say that?"

"Because you already changed mine."

With that, he was gone.

Later, she sat at her kitchen table, scrolling through the comments.

*Isn't this just Sam's shadow?*

*Wake up, ladies. Same hustle, new lipstick.*

*Another puppet pretending to be a prophet.*

Autumn's hand hovered over the keyboard. Brooklyn slid her a mug of tea.

"They're loud, but not the whole story," Brooklyn said gently.

"I want to tell them the truth," Autumn whispered. "But what if they only hear the noise?"

Brooklyn nodded.

"Then we keep showing up. Because authenticity doesn't compete, it survives."

Autumn considered the last seven days. She scanned her journal for reminders. The first day was chaos. She'd bumped into Marcus near the courthouse. He brought coffee and told her, "I'm not just investigating a case. I'm watching a woman rebuild her soul in real time."

Day two was silent. There were no calls and no content. She realized she hated stillness because it demanded honesty. The third day brought memories that washed over her without reprieve. She thought of her father's distance and her mother's pride. She cried alone in luxury silk pajamas, ashamed that money never made her whole. By the fourth day, she was confused and chose to write a letter to God. *I'm angry. I feel betrayed. I don't know what I'm doing. Show me who I am when no one's watching.*

On day five she had a dream. She walked on cracked ground, holding broken glass. Women gathered beside her and built a mosaic from the shards. In the center was a throne with a crown made of glass.

Autumn wore it.

On day six, Serenity brought Sam's journal and Autumn knew she could never again trust anyone who asked her to bury her truth.

Day seven came with vision. The name came to her: Billionaire Broke Girls. It was not just a brand. It was a calling, a community, a rebirth.

That evening, as candles flickered and gospel hummed, Autumn stood in front of the mirror. She didn't see Sam's shadow. She didn't see shame. She saw herself. Whole, holy, and healing.

# PART IV

## THE BLUEPRINT

# CHAPTER TEN

# Build from the Bones

Autumn stepped out of her favorite coffee shop, still clutching the sleeve of her warm beverage like it was armor. The street was quiet, but a shadow shifted just beyond the streetlight's reach.

Her steps quickened. Not from the chill in the air but from something ancient. Instinct. A warning.

Then, "Hey."

Marcus's voice was low and calm, yet it made her jump. He was suddenly at her side, emerging from the darkness like a guardian angel in black.

"You okay?" he asked, watching her closely.

She shook her head. "I felt...watched. Not by God or grief but something else."

Marcus scanned the street like a trained soldier.

"Caleb's threats aren't just words. He's unraveling. I've seen it before."

"I know." Her voice trembled. "I just didn't think it would feel this close."

"You're not walking through this alone," he said, stepping closer. "I mean it."

Autumn looked up, finally meeting his eyes. "Thank you. I'm scared, Marcus."

He reached for her hand, lacing their fingers without hesitation.

"Then be scared. Just don't stop moving."

Her body remembered something her soul was still learning. Fear isn't always a stop sign. Sometimes, it's the sound of destiny knocking.

* * *

That night, the silence inside Brooklyn's guest room felt like a sanctuary. The fast had stripped everything away. No wine. No phone. No distractions. Just water, scripture, and silence. Autumn sat cross-legged on the floor, wrapped in her favorite knit shawl like a prayer cloth. A single candle flickered beside her, its flame dancing in rhythm with her breath. Before her, resting like something sacred, was Samantha's journal.

She hadn't opened it since the last breakdown. Since discovering the forged contracts. Since realizing Samantha Monroe—mentor, mogul, murderer's mother—had been a mirage and a mirror all at once.

But tonight, something shifted. She reached for it slowly, reverently, like it might still bleed. The worn leather cover still held its shape. The gold-foil initials shimmered beneath the candlelight. Inside, folded carefully, was a note in Sam's delicate cursive, *If I die before I heal, forgive me anyway.*

Autumn inhaled sharply. Her hands trembled as she flipped to the final pages. The ink was messy. Raw. No longer Sam's flawless, curated script.

**Journal Entry**
**August 3rd — 2:14 a.m.**

*I don't know who this is for. Maybe Breezy. Maybe God. Maybe the little girl in me is still trying to win love with power plays and Prada pumps. I built my empire on perception, not purpose. Now it crumbles like the lie it was.*

*Breezy trusted me. I used that trust to manipulate, to survive. I forged her name. I used her voice. I feared the light she carried would expose my rot.*

*If she ever finds this, tell her I didn't mean to destroy her. I was just trying to survive.*

*But legacy doesn't live in survival. It lives in surrender.*

Autumn closed her eyes, the pain twisting fresh in her gut. When she opened them again, she turned to the next page. There, scrawled in thick ink:

*There's danger in her path. But glory too. God will use her to tear down what I built...and raise something holy.*

A sob escaped her lips, silent and sudden. Sam hadn't just used her, she'd seen her. Even if it's too late.

Brooklyn entered quietly, holding a Bible in one hand and a cup of turmeric tea in the other.

"That Sam?" she asked softly, kneeling beside her.

Autumn nodded, her throat tight.

Brooklyn scanned the words on the open page.

"She was warning you."

"She knew. She saw it coming."

Brooklyn reached over, squeezing her hand gently.

"Even Judas kissed Jesus," she said. "Don't get lost in betrayal, Breezy. Focus on resurrection."

Autumn smiled through the ache. Sam had died broken, but not blind. Now it was Autumn's turn to rise.

The next morning, vision returned. She pinned her mood board to the wall. On it were colors, quotes, silhouettes of women laughing in resilience. In bold Sharpie, she scrawled across the top: **Billionaire Broke Girls.**

The first brunch was set. Serenity agreed to open with a spoken word prayer. Hazel secured a historic Black-owned venue in uptown Charlotte. Brooklyn designed T-shirts that read: **Built from the Break.**

But as vision grew, so did resistance. Emails glitched. A vendor ghosted. A fraudulent bank transaction was flagged under *Autumn B. James.*

Then came the flowers. A bouquet of white hydrangeas appeared on her doorstep. No card. No note. Just fragrance and memory. Sam's signature.

* * *

The venue was buzzing with Black excellence, heels clicking, lashes fluttering, eyes watching.

Autumn stood by the refreshment table when a woman approached with a tight smile and a tailored blazer.

"Autumn James?"

"Yes," Autumn replied cautiously.

"I'm Diane. I worked under Samantha Monroe before...before it all fell apart. I lost my savings in one of her fake property deals."

Autumn's stomach dropped.

"I'm so sorry you went through that. I really am."

"And now you're reviving her brand?" Diane's voice cut like a blade. "Seriously?"

"It's not *her* brand," Autumn said, standing taller. "Billionaire Broke Girls is something new, built on truth and healing."

Diane scoffed. "Sounds like damage control."

Before Autumn could speak again, Hazel stepped beside her like a shield.

"We're committed to accountability," Hazel said calmly. "This isn't the resurrection of Sam. It's a reclamation for everyone she hurt."

Autumn took a breath. Her voice found itself again.

"I don't expect trust overnight," she said, eyes locked with Diane's. "But I do invite it. Healing isn't PR. It's personal, and we're starting with honesty."

Diane didn't reply. But something flickered behind her eyes. Not anger. Maybe consideration.

Later that evening, as Autumn scrolled through the RSVP list for the brunch, one name stopped her cold. J. Monroe +1.

Her chest tightened. Jerald?

She hadn't seen him since Samantha's funeral. Could it really be him? And if not him, then who?

* * *

The sunlight poured through the co-working space's tall windows, dancing across reclaimed wood desks and vision boards.

"This," Autumn said, standing before Hazel and Brooklyn, "is where legacy begins."

Hazel smirked, adjusting her glasses.

"You've got vision. Now let's build the structure to hold it."

For months, Hazel had become more than a lawyer. She was a fortress, guiding Autumn through contracts, incorporation requirements, and boundaries.

"A business without structure," Hazel warned, "is a ship without a rudder. Either you steer, or it steers you off a cliff."

"I'm ready," Autumn said. "Let's build."

That evening, the *Billionaire Broke Girls Brunch* opened to a packed room.

"This," she said, catching Autumn's eye, "is how real wealth looks."

Autumn breathed in an air of community, courage, and calling. The space had women from all backgrounds, all stories. They were all sisters and survivors. Laughter and tears shared the same space. Testimonies spilled like oil on a prophet's altar.

Autumn stood before them, heart pounding. She was no longer a broken executive in hiding. She was a builder.

"We are not defined by our scars or our silence," she said. "We are defined by how we rise. By the legacy we choose to build."

She scanned the crowd of strangers, friends, and maybe even enemies, bound by one thing: hope.

* * *

The week before the brunch, Autumn found herself driving toward the one place she'd promised never to return without armor—her grandmother's house.

She hadn't planned to stop.

She told herself it was to say goodbye to the magnolia tree in the front yard and to the dent in the porch rail where she and Brooklyn used to launch jump ropes like slingshots. But when she pulled up, the living room curtains were open. The front door cracked just enough to show Aretha's silhouette, swaying slowly like a memory that wouldn't leave.

Autumn sat in the car, fingers frozen on the key. She could've backed out of the driveway and left the past where it belonged. But something in her, maybe grief, maybe God, wouldn't let her.

She parked and stepped out of the car. The gravel crunched under her boots as she made her way up the steps. The old screen door groaned like it remembered everything.

Aretha didn't look up from where she sat at the kitchen table, peeling sweet potatoes with short, careful strokes.

"Well," she said, not unkindly. "Look what the cat drug back."

Autumn lingered at the doorway.

"You always did know how to make a person feel at home."

Aretha dropped a potato in the bowl.

"What are you here for, girl? Ain't no more ghosts need stirring."

"I came to say goodbye," Autumn said, stepping into the kitchen. The house still smelled like rose oil and mothballs. "It's being sold next week."

Aretha's hands paused. "So, it's really happening?"

"It's time." Autumn's voice softened. "Granny's gone. The house...it isn't what holds her."

Aretha wiped her hands on a dish towel and sighed.

"You always were the one to get out. Guess I just didn't think you'd come back and tear everything down in the process."

Autumn blinked. "I didn't tear anything down. I uncovered it. There's a difference."

Finally, Aretha looked at her, and for once, her eyes weren't full of fight. Just fatigue.

"You think that makes you better than us?" she asked. "You walk around talkin' about healing and God and purpose like them wounds didn't start right here in this kitchen."

Autumn inhaled deeply.

"I don't think I'm better. I think I was broken, and I got tired of pretending I wasn't."

A long silence stretched between them, hanging like unspoken laundry.

Aretha pulled out a second chair with her foot. "Well, sit if you got a minute. Potatoes don't peel themselves."

Autumn sat. For a while, the only sounds were the scrapes of knives against skins. A rhythm. A ritual.

Aretha spoke first. "You remember that time you told me I was a squatter in my own mama's house?"

Autumn winced. "I remember."

"I wanted to slap the taste out your mouth," Aretha chuckled, shaking her head. "But I knew you were right. Just couldn't say it out loud then."

"I was angry," Autumn admitted. "Grief made everything feel like an attack."

Aretha nodded. "Grief ain't picky. It pickpockets everybody."

A crooked smile crept across Autumn's face.

"I'm sorry, Auntie."

Aretha paused. "Me too."

They kept peeling. The bowl between them filled slowly, like time. Like mercy.

"I think I needed to know," Autumn said finally, "that forgiveness doesn't mean forgetting. That I could still honor Granny without letting her silence be my own."

Aretha blinked at her.

"Girl, who taught you to talk like that?"

Autumn laughed softly. "Therapy and Jesus. In that order."

Aretha let out a raspy laugh that sounded like cigarette smoke and secrets.

"Well, both of 'em are doing their job."

Autumn looked up. "So...we good?"

Aretha leaned back. "We're getting there."

Autumn reached into her purse and unfolded a worn photo of her Granny flanked by a young Aretha and Marlene, Autumn's mom, in pigtails. All three held tambourines and stood in their Sunday best outside New Zion Missionary Baptist.

"Thought you might want this."

Aretha took it like it was a relic. "Thank you."

Autumn stood. "I'll leave the key on the table."

"Don't," Aretha said quickly. "Keep it. Every woman needs to know she got the keys to her own story."

Autumn stopped at the door, surprised.

"Make that legacy count, Breezy," Aretha whispered.

Autumn froze. She turned slowly.

"What did you just call me?"

"That's what mama used to call you. Breezy. Said you blew through people's lives like wind, messy, healing, hard to catch. I figured it's time somebody else said it, too."

Autumn swallowed the lump in her throat.

"Thanks."

She stepped out into the sunlight.

This time, the road didn't feel so heavy.

# CHAPTER ELEVEN

# Boardrooms Without Walls

The morning air smelled like fresh rain and possibility. At the edge of Brooklyn's neighborhood park, the grass shimmered with dew, and the rhythm of quiet hustle pulsed through the space. Vendors arranged candles and waist beads, elders folded chairs with practiced grace, and kids chased oversized bubbles across the lawn. It wasn't a boardroom. But today, it was the birthplace of something real.

Autumn stood under the pop-up canopy, watching as a wide circle of tables came to life. Cloth napkins printed with scripture fluttered in the breeze. Proverbs 31:25 on some. Isaiah 61:3 on others. The phrase *wealth begins within* was hand-lettered on the welcome sign, not as a slogan, but a promise.

The women came in layers, hoodies and heels, church hats and work boots. Some held resumes in tan folders. Others clutched toddlers or side-eyes full of caution. All of them bore the same glassy-eyed look of hope, muted by pain.

Brooklyn stepped beside Autumn, eyes scanning the crowd. "This is it," she whispered. "This is what boardrooms without walls really looks like."

Autumn adjusted her mic, inhaling the moment.

"Let's begin." She stepped forward into the circle.

"Welcome, Queens," she said, voice steady but soft. "Today, we tear down walls to build something sacred. No jargon. No judgment. Just truth. Just us."

A hand shot up near the front, a woman with silver-streaked locs, her face lined with grit and grace.

"How do you build wealth," she asked, "when all you've ever known is survival?"

Autumn placed a hand over her own heart.

"It starts right here," she answered. "Your worth isn't in hustle. It's not in bank accounts or college degrees. It's in the God who made you. The God who kept you alive when systems failed you."

Murmurs of agreement rippled through the circle.

She told her story, the exhaustion from performing, the betrayal that cost her everything, the therapist who told her she wasn't crazy for feeling broken, the moment she began to rise.

Serenity moved quietly through the crowd, offering whispered prayers and gentle affirmations. Hazel answered questions about business ownership, contracts, and trademarks. Brooklyn, ever the flame, ignited hope with humor and strategy.

A woman named Lila stood to speak.

"I lost everything—my kids, my freedom, my dignity. But when I found God in a jail cell, I found a new beginning. He broke me before He remade me."

The women clapped, cried, and rose to their feet.

Later, a weary-eyed mother shared through tear-stained cheeks how medical bills and credit card debt forced her to shutter the hair salon she once dreamed would carry her family.

Autumn met her gaze across the circle. "Healing doesn't erase the scars," she said. "But it teaches us how to dance in the rain."

The crowd exhaled. Some laughed. Some wept. But no one left unchanged.

Business ideas were scribbled on paper bags. Phone numbers exchanged like sacred seeds. Promises were whispered over plates of food. This wasn't a seminar. It was a spiritual reset.

As the sun dipped behind the oaks, Autumn saw him near the edge of the event, Detective Marcus, in jeans and a gray t-shirt, hands in his pockets, eyes trained only on her.

He waited until the crowd thinned before approaching.

"You're the real deal," he said.

Autumn smiled, surprised by how deeply those words landed.

"And you're still showing up," she replied.

He shrugged. "Because you're worth showing up for."

Before she could respond, Brooklyn bounded over, her curls bouncing with joy. She slung an arm around Autumn's shoulders and leaned in.

"This? This is your kingdom now."

Autumn looked around at the women packing up, the prayers still lingering in the air like perfume. There was no boardroom. No glass ceiling. Just open sky and open hearts.

That night, the house was quiet except for the rhythmic hum of the dishwasher and the soft creak of the wood floor beneath Hazel's feet.

She placed a glass of water in front of Autumn and sat beside her on the couch.

"You're carrying more than just a business," Hazel said gently. "This is legacy. Reputation. Trauma. All of it, braided together."

Autumn slumped forward, head in hands.

"Some days I wonder if I'm the right person to lead this. Maybe someone else could've done it cleaner."

Serenity appeared from the hallway, barefoot and calm, drawn by the weight in the room. She lowered herself beside the fireplace, pulling her knees to her chest.

"You're not leading alone," she said softly. "Plus, leadership is never about perfection. It's about showing up, again and again, even when it's messy."

Autumn leaned back, closing her eyes.

"I want to believe that. I really do."

Brooklyn's laughter floated from the kitchen. It was light and unbothered, like a hymn reminding them of joy.

Hazel smiled faintly. "Your grandmother would've said the same. Strength isn't loud, it's layered."

Serenity reached for Autumn's hand. "The resistance is real. But so is your calling."

Later that night, Hazel stood alone by the window, looking out at the city, lost in her own memory.

It had been years since she first met Samantha Monroe. Back when Monroe Beauty Bar was nothing more than a dream in a worn-out notebook.

They had met over tea at a café in Charlotte. Sam was magnetic, equal parts brilliance and bravado.

"I want to build something that makes women feel powerful again," Sam had said.

Hazel had believed her. Back then, they'd laughed like sisters as they compared notes on boardroom microaggressions and bad dates with good-looking liars. Hazel had helped her incorporate her first business and draft her first trademark application.

But over time, the deals grew murkier.

Hazel remembered the day Samantha slid a nondisclosure agreement across the table, worded in a way that silenced victims more than it protected ideas.

"I can't draft this," Hazel had said, pushing it back.

Sam's eyes turned cold. "You're either with me or in my way."

While Hazel had walked away that day, her guilt never did. Now, with Autumn stepping into the fire Sam left behind, Hazel felt the ache of a sister she couldn't save, and the sacred responsibility to protect the one still standing.

# CHAPTER TWELVE

# Bloodlines & Blessings

Autumn's phone buzzed sharply on the counter. Before she answered, a notification flashed across the screen telling her she'd missed a call from her mom.

Autumn stared at it, her pulse racing. Then it buzzed again but this time, she picked up.

"Autumn," her mother's voice came quiet, uncertain. "Can I come see you?"

There it was, the crossroad.

"Yes," Autumn said carefully. "But...why now?"

Her mother exhaled. "Because life's too short, and I want to heal what I broke."

The knock came before Autumn was ready.

She sat cross-legged on her grandmother's old couch, journal open but untouched. Her mind waded through prayers, flashbacks, and the sharp ache of what never was.

The door creaked.

Marlene Brees stood in the doorway, still graceful, still guarded, but softened by time.

"Mom."

"Hey, baby."

They sat across from one another like old photographs.

"I'm sorry I wasn't there," Marlene said, tears clinging to her voice. "I thought I was doing the right thing. But I was wrong."

"You should've been there, Mom," Autumn whispered. "But you weren't."

Marlene fumbled in her purse and pulled out a faded photo of Autumn as a child, laughing in a sunbeam. "I disappeared because I thought success meant sacrifice. I thought if I left, you'd be better off."

Autumn's voice cracked. "But I needed *you*. Not your ambition. Just you."

They sat in silence until Autumn finally said what needed to be said.

"I forgive you. But I need honesty. And I need you to *stay*. No more disappearing."

"I'm here now," Marlene said, nodding slowly. "If you'll let me be."

By night's end, they stood at the door again.

"Your grandmother used to say, 'Blood is thicker when it's healed.' I want to be part of that healing."

Autumn took her hand.

"I want that too."

She watched her mother walk into the night, toward the unknown, but not away.

She whispered, "Thank you, God, for this blessing wrapped in brokenness."

Just as the house began to settle, the door burst open.

Aretha stood in the doorway, face flushed, an envelope clutched in her hand.

"You need to see this," she said, breathless.

She tossed it onto the table. Autumn picked it up carefully. Inside was a copy of Samantha's autopsy report. The cause of death was listed as cardiac arrest due to a prescription interaction.

It also listed an unofficial suspicion of possible foul play.

Autumn's fingers trembled.

"Where did you get this?"

"Mail slot," Aretha replied. "No return address."

Brooklyn, who had ridden over with Aretha, stepped closer, took the paper, and read it slowly.

"This ain't no accident," she said. "This is either a warning or a clue."

Autumn looked out the window, past the porch, into the dark.

"Someone wants us to start asking questions." She tightened her grip on the file. "And now, we will."

* * *

Six weeks before Samantha's death, rain tapped against the floor-to-ceiling windows like it was trying to warn them. Autumn stood near the glass, arms crossed, eyes scanning Charlotte's skyline. Samantha sat curled on her velvet chaise, phone in one hand, wine in the other, scrolling headlines that mentioned neither of their names, yet.

"Do you ever think we flew too close to the sun?" Autumn asked, her voice low, almost reverent.

Samantha looked up, surprised.

"That's what we do, Breezy. We build wings out of strategy and stardust. You just mad they noticed how high we got."

Autumn turned. "It's not that. It's just...I don't know who I am outside of all this. Outside of your vision."

Samantha stood, her robe dragging like a veil behind her. She walked over slowly, placing her hands on Autumn's shoulders.

"You're my legacy. That's who you are."

Something in Autumn flinched. A flicker of unease passed between them, but Samantha smoothed it away with a practiced smile.

"You don't think I handpicked you by accident, do you? You were hungry enough to lead, but obedient enough to learn. You gave me hope that one of us would make it out clean."

Autumn blinked. "Clean? Sam, are we in something I don't know about?"

Samantha tilted her head, then chuckled. "Baby, you don't win like this by being clean."

The words hit hard. Autumn took a step back.

"Have you done something I should be worried about?"

"Worry is for women who don't know how to pivot," Samantha replied, now sipping her wine like it was communion. "And you, my dear, are the pivot."

Autumn felt her chest tighten. "I trusted you with my name, my accounts, my clients!"

"And I gave you a platform, prestige, and power," Samantha snapped, eyes flaring. "Let's not pretend it was charity."

Autumn grabbed her coat. "This doesn't feel like a partnership anymore. It feels like...property or pity or something worse."

"You'll understand one day," Samantha said very matter-of-factly. "Sometimes power moves through people. Sometimes we're just vessels."

Autumn paused at the door.

"Vessels don't lie to the people they pour into."

Their eyes met. Something ancient and broken passed between them. Autumn left, slamming the door on both the storm outside and the storm she couldn't yet name inside.

# PART V

## THE BIRTH

# CHAPTER THIRTEEN

# When the Bag Finds You

Samantha Monroe's former office was colder than Hazel remembered. Gutted of glamour and stripped of seduction, it was merely four walls and too many ghosts.

She stood in the silence, clutching the worn file folder that hadn't left her bag since the night Samantha's memorial ended in whispers instead of peace.

The door creaked behind her. Hazel spoke without turning.

"I knew you'd show up."

Caleb Monroe leaned against the frame, the overhead light catching on his cufflinks. Impeccable. Untouched. Calculated.

"You always did like playing detective."

Hazel turned, "No, I like the truth. You? You've been allergic to it since high school."

He stepped into the room, shutting the door behind him like he owned the building. Like his mother hadn't left it to someone else.

"So, what now? You're gonna cry conspiracy and wave around your little folder?"

"This isn't theory. This is evidence of forged contracts, hidden transfers, and a draft will to cut you out completely."

That silenced him.

Hazel circled the desk, slow and intentional.

"She changed everything and left it all to Autumn. Not even a shred of paper for you, Caleb."

His jaw twitched.

"I watched her try to protect you until she couldn't protect herself. You want to know the saddest part?"

Caleb didn't answer. He didn't have to.

Hazel continued. "She was afraid of you."

Caleb stepped forward.

"You don't know what you're talking about."

"I know enough. She left this in case something ever happened." She held up a file. Caleb's eyes flickered. After a few seconds, he smiled.

"You're reaching, counselor."

"And you're unraveling."

They stared at each other. A standoff of grief, guilt, and power.

Caleb stepped closer to remove the distance between them.

"Be careful, Ms. Youngblood. Some graves are better left undisturbed."

Unflinching, Hazel replied, "But some legacies demand resurrection."

He smirked, turned, and left. The door clicked shut behind him.

Hazel's hands trembled now that she was alone. She opened the folder again, just to make sure the truth was still there. A single note in Samantha's sharp handwriting slid loose.

*"If he ever comes looking for what I stole, remind him I never took what wasn't already mine."*

Hazel pressed a hand to her chest.

"God help us. It's starting."

* * *

Early the next morning, Autumn sat hunched over her laptop. The only light in the room came from her screen as the sunrise slowly cut through the windows. Her phone buzzed with a text from Brooklyn.

*Big client calling. Are you ready?*

Autumn took a deep breath and dialed into the meeting.

"Hi, Autumn. This is Lila from GreenLeaf Organics. We've been watching you and love your journey and the soul work you're doing. We'd love to have you on board."

Autumn, somewhat stunned, took a second to reply.

"Thank you. I'd love that."

No begging. No performance. Just the truth. Conviction over convincing. Just like Serenity had taught her.

That evening at Brooklyn's townhome, wine glasses clinked over a table scattered with contracts, vision boards, and candlelight.

Brooklyn gave a toast. "To when the bag finds *you*."

"To legacy over leverage," added Autumn with a knowing smile.

They drank deep.

Brooklyn paused and set down her glass.

"Hmmm...Sam would've hated this." Then she grinned and winked. "Which means we're doing it right!"

* * *

Later that week, Autumn sat on the velvet couch, Marcus at her side, as her salt lamp glowed in the corner. Hazel stood by the bookshelf, motionless.

Finally, Hazel spoke. "I should've said something sooner."

"Said what?" asked Marcus.

Hazel moved closer, her voice barely above a whisper.

"Caleb. Samantha brought me on to help clean up her business but Caleb was already there. Quiet. Angry. Watching everything."

Autumn leaned forward.

Hazel continued. "He hated her for choosing the brand over bedtime. He never forgave her for sending him away. When she started shifting her will, including you, Autumn, I knew there would be trouble."

"He always looked at me like I didn't belong." Autumn looked at her hands in her lap.

"You weren't just in his way. You were her choice," said Hazel.

"Given everything you know, do you think he did it?" Marcus looked at Hazel with a raised brow.

Hazel didn't answer. Instead, she handed Autumn the folder with Samantha's notes, financial records, and drafts of new trusts and estate plans.

Autumn read aloud.

*"If I die before I can tell Autumn the truth, let these pages speak louder than my silence ever could."*

The room fell silent.

Marcus rose. "I'll subpoena Jerald's financials. If Caleb's tied to them, we'll find a trail."

Hazel added, "I'll file to freeze her estate." She gripped Autumn's hand. "This isn't just about Samantha. This is about every woman who's ever been lied to by someone they trusted."

Autumn nodded. "Then I'll finish what she started and make sure Caleb never profits from her pain."

"I'll pick him up for questioning." Marcus was halfway to the door.

A lawyer, a detective, and a daughter-by-choice were on a mission from God.

* * *

Caleb sat in the dark of Samantha's estate, bourbon in hand. A single photo of Samantha glared up at him. He turned it face down. *She should've left well enough alone.*

From the shadows, her voice echoed in his memory. *"You don't inherit love by force, Caleb. You inherit legacy through healing."*

The glass shattered in his fist.

From outside, headlights approached. Detective Marcus had arrived and this time, the truth would not be buried.

* * *

Hazel's first meeting with Samantha was under fluorescent lights and tension.

Samantha sighed. "Let me guess, you're gonna tell me not to mix my personal and business accounts?"

Hazel smirked. "No. I'm going to tell you I won't cover it up if you do."

They stared at each other. Then laughed.

Samantha admitted, "You're dangerous. I like that."

But years later, the tension returned when Hazel refused to draft an exploitative NDA. Samantha cut her off without a word.

Hazel had always wondered if that was the day she sacrificed her silence or saved her soul. When Hazel saw Sam's journal entry dated two weeks before her death, she knew the answer.

*"Hazel won't lie for me anymore. That's how I know she still has a moral compass. I'm scared for what Caleb might do, but if I run, I'll only leave Autumn with the pieces. She's strong. But not invincible. I just pray the Lord tells her where the landmines are."*

# CHAPTER FOURTEEN

# Legacy Over Likes

The late sun filtered through the tall windows of Hazel Youngblood's law firm, casting golden stripes across the floor like prison bars. Autumn sat curled in Hazel's oversized velvet chair, legs tucked under her, journal open in her lap. Her eyes were stiff, equal parts exhaustion and disbelief.

Hazel sat across from her, not as lead counsel, but as something older, heavier. A keeper of truth.

Autumn's voice cracked the quiet, "None of this adds up. Sam said she wanted me to take over BBG. She referenced the brand's mission in her journal but we didn't start BBG until *after* she passed. Or at least, I thought we didn't."

She turned to Serenity, seated quietly on the couch nearby.

Autumn continued, "When did all of this *really* begin?"

Hazel leaned forward, calm and deliberate.

"That's what we need to talk about. You're not crazy, Autumn. You've just been swimming in waves Sam started long before she was gone."

She reached into her leather bag and pulled out a thin manila folder.

"I didn't want to show you this until you were ready."

Autumn straightened. "Show me what?"

"A timeline. One I pieced together from Sam's filings, old emails, therapy notes she gave me permission to archive, and the truth she never told you."

Hazel handed over a printed sheet, color-coded, full of names, dates, and tiny arrows connecting secrets.

"You should start at the beginning."

### 2017: The Mixer

Hazel narrated. "You two first met at that women entrepreneur mixer. Sam was already developing early concepts for a brand called *Wealth Made Well*. That was the prototype for BBG."

"She never told me that," Autumn said almost inaudibly.

### 2018: The Hustle

"She started quietly trademarking phrases and filed an LLC with *your* name listed as future co-founder. But you never knew."

Autumn's eyes flew up, stunned. "She filed legal paperwork *with my name*, and never told me?"

"She was building you into her vision, without giving you the wheel. That's how control looks when it dresses up as mentorship."

### 2019: Introduction to Serenity

"She referred you to Serenity after the panic attacks started."

Serenity gently added, "At first, I thought it was just therapy. But I can admit that I saw signs, Autumn. Emotional manipulation wrapped in affirmation."

### 2020: Sam's Personal Breakdown

"She began pulling money from shell companies. Companies connected to BBG, all hidden under the original Wealth Made Well umbrella."

"So, she wanted BBG to be both ministry and misdirection?" Autumn asked as her breath quickened.

### Early 2021: Brings Caleb into the Business

"She brought her son into the business quietly. He was introduced as a tech consultant, but he was accessing accounts, yours included," Hazel said to Autumn.

Serenity added, "She didn't trust you to hold what she was building. She was terrified you'd leave her."

"She built it *for* me, without me, and then broke it before I ever had the chance?"

Hazel nodded.

"Exactly."

### Late 2021: Obvious Signs

Hazel turned to a highlighted journal entry.

*"I thought she'd never find out. But Autumn is light. You can't bury light in shadows forever. I'm praying Caleb stays in his lane. He has my temper, not my faith."*

"So she *knew* Caleb was spiraling?" asked Autumn.

"And she didn't stop him," added Serenity.

### February 2022: Samantha's Death

The folder lay open like a wound.

"They said it was an accident. But Sam's fear wasn't misplaced." Serenity spoke what they were all thinking.

"Do you really think Caleb...?" Autumn wondered aloud.

Hazel didn't answer. She just closed the file.

### *2023: BBG Reborn*

"Wait, what is this about BBG?" Autumn asked, confused.

"You didn't launch BBG, you *resurrected* it. It was buried beneath betrayal. But it's always been your mantle." Serenity's words provided a hint of solace for the spiraling thoughts inside Autumn's head and heart.

Autumn's hand trembled as she folded the paper.

"So, I'm not losing my mind?"

Hazel responded, "No. You're uncovering what was always there." Hazel took Autumn's hand firmly.

"What you do with that truth now, Autumn, is everything."

* * *

## Present Day

Autumn stood onstage, blazer crisp, the words *"Perception is Price. Purpose is Power."* stitched across her back.

She approached the mic, her voice steady.

"This is our movement, Billionaire Broke Girls. Flawed and flourishing because we choose healing over hiding."

Brooklyn beamed from the front. Serenity and Hazel stood like twin pillars beside her.

As Autumn scanned the crowd, she abruptly stopped. At the back sat a young man. Clean fade. Designer sneakers. Jawline sharp and *familiar*. He watched her, eyes locked, unmoving.

The crowd rose, napkins lifted, *Flawed but Flourishing* printed in gold. As the music swelled, Autumn stepped aside.

Autumn's mother stood silently by the green room door, unsure. Autumn met her gaze and nodded, inviting her in. Later, they sat together in a quiet corner. No words. Just hands held.

Moments later, Hazel burst in, pacing with a phone to her ear.

"They're moving forward with the audit. Caleb's name is linked to two shell accounts. Money left *before* Samantha died."

"Does Marcus know?" Autumn asked, ready to make the call.

"Yes, he's already briefing the DA."

Autumn looked down at her journal. *God doesn't just vindicate. He elevates.*

The room was nearly empty now as staff folded chairs and discarded most of the decorations. Autumn grabbed the sign-in sheet from the welcome table. She scanned it until she found his name. Caleb Monroe.

Her hands clenched the paper. "He was here."

Brooklyn tensed. "I didn't even see him. Did he say anything? Where was he?"

"He was in the back. He didn't say anything. Just watched."

They stood in silence.

"Brooklyn, Sam didn't die of a heart condition."

"Then we'd better prepare for more than a brand launch," Brooklyn replied only half-jokingly.

* * *

Bright lights bathed the minimalist stage in soft gold. A single white armchair faced its match across a glass coffee table. The audience was hushed as the camera blinked red. Keisha Ray, elegant in a structured red suit, adjusted her mic and leaned in with her signature velvet intensity.

"Autumn Brees James, once a whispered name, linked to scandal, secrets, and silence, is now being shouted from pulpits and platforms across the country. Tell me, what changed?"

Autumn sat upright with unclenched hands folded in her lap. "Grief changed me. Betrayal woke me. God rebuilt me."

A ripple of tension traveled through the audience. Keisha's brow arched slightly. She turned a page on her notepad, slowly, deliberately.

"Let's discuss your former mentor, Samantha Monroe. Her death wasn't just a headline. It was a storm. Her son, Caleb, remains shrouded in suspicion. Some say money vanished. Others say power shifted. Autumn, how do you move forward when your past still stalks you?"

Autumn steadied her breath, locking eyes with the camera.

"You rewrite the story. You tell the truth. You make sure the next chapter heals the reader, not just the writer."

A hush fell over the studio. Even the camera crew stopped moving. For a moment, the weight of it all, Sam's betrayal, the broken trust, the blood, hung in the air like incense.

* * *

High above Charlotte, the skyline bled into dusk through crystal glass. Inside, dim light flickered from a wall-mounted TV. Caleb Monroe sat slouched in a black leather armchair, sipping a bourbon on the rocks. The BBG interview was on the screen.

He watched silently as Autumn's face filled the screen. Her calm unnerved him. Her poise felt like a verdict.

The ice in his glass cracked loudly, too loudly in the quiet.

*Bzzzzzz...*

He glanced down at the phone glowing beside him. An unknown number flashed. He lifted the phone and unlocked the screen.

> ***It's unraveling. We warned you.***

He replied without flinching.

> *Handle it.*

The response came immediately.

> *There's nothing left to handle. Hazel turned over the accounts. Detective King's team confirmed the signatures. The journals are going to press. We're out of time.*

Caleb's throat tightened. He placed the glass on the mahogany side table, hard. He stood, turned away from the TV, and walked slowly toward the built-in bookshelf that lined the far wall.

After a few minutes, his eyes found it, like muscle memory, on the lacquered panel halfway down, hiding behind old business books and a fake statuette. He knelt. The door slid back to reveal a small safe embedded in the wall. The same safe Samantha had told him, more than once, never to touch.

His fingers hovered over the keypad. He hesitated, then entered the date of his parents' divorce.

*Beep!*

The lock disengaged.

Inside, a stack of documents sat wrapped in velvet ribbon. A flash drive. A silver cross necklace. And beneath it all, a single white envelope with a note: *For Autumn, if she ever asks.*

Caleb's face darkened. His breath caught. She never trusted him. Not fully. Not even in death.

For the first time, he realized just how much she had left behind.

# CHAPTER FIFTEEN

# The Vault

Autumn stood in front of the climate-controlled storage unit, her breath caught between courage and collapse. The brushed-gold envelope had come days ago with no return address, just a Winston-Salem postmark and a single, gleaming key.

Everything in her body screamed *Turn back,* but something deeper whispered, *Keep going.*

Hazel stood beside her, quiet but alert, her purse slung cross-body with a discreet Glock tucked inside. She scanned the lot, sharp eyes slicing through dusk.

Brooklyn waited nearby, engine humming, watching the rearview like a hawk. Her hand stayed close to her phone, ready to call if things went sideways.

"You sure you wanna do this?" Hazel asked hesitantly.

"No," Autumn murmured, her hand trembling as it hovered near the lock. "But I have to."

With a deep inhale, she turned the key. The metal door let out a groan. As it creaked open, a chill seeped out. Not just cold, but...*intentional.* It was as though something had been waiting.

Inside, the unit stretched long and narrow, lit by a single flickering overhead bulb. Dozens of boxes lined the metal shelves, labeled in crisp, clinical handwriting.

*S.M. ARCHIVES: Contracts. Photos. Sermon Notes. Financials.*

But one box stood apart. It was taped shut and labeled in jagged black marker: *Caleb Monroe*.

Autumn stepped forward, heart hammering. She crouched, hands gingerly pulling the box toward her. Inside, she discovered a flood of papers that included police reports, psychiatric evaluations, and sealed court records. At the bottom, tucked inside a worn leather journal, was a flash drive labeled JUST IN CASE.

Hazel dropped to one knee beside her, pulled a sleek black laptop from her bag, and booted it up.

"You ready?" she asked once the flash drive was inserted.

"No," Autumn whispered again as she eyed the video file staring back at them. "But push play."

A grainy image of Samantha Monroe filled the frame. Her hair was pulled into a messy bun. She wore no makeup to cover her swollen and red-rimmed eyes. Her skin was pale and lifeless, as though fear wrapped around her like a second skin.

"If you're watching this...then something went wrong."

Autumn held her breath.

"I always knew Caleb had darkness in him. But I didn't know how far it would go. I...I tried...I tried so hard."

She looked off-camera, eyes darting like she expected someone to burst in at any moment.

"He found out about the files. About the things I kept on people. About the ones I kept...on him. The blackmail. The leverage. Everything." Her voice cracked.

"I was trying to protect the legacy...protect BBG. Protect *you*. But if he's watching this, too, Caleb, you broke something sacred. If anything happens to me, don't let him charm you. Don't let him rewrite the story." She paused, voice barely a whisper now.

"I didn't birth a monster...but I might've created one."

The screen cut to black.

Hazel's breath came slow and shaky.

"She knew," she whispered. "And she was terrified."

Autumn stared at the laptop, the silence around her suddenly deafening.

"Now he knows that we know." She reached back into the box, pulling out a sealed folder labeled *Legal, BBG Transfers & Payoffs*.

Autumn didn't open it, she just held it. She pressed it against her chest like a weight she didn't know she'd been carrying all this time.

The overhead bulb buzzed.

Outside, the city lights of Charlotte blinked in the distance, like quiet witnesses. But here, in this vault of secrets, truth breathed loud and sharp.

Autumn sat on the cold concrete, her voice slow but resolute.

"So, I was chosen before I knew I was chosen. Then manipulated...before I even knew I was worthy?"

Hazel looked at her, fierce and soft at the same time. "Yes."

Autumn's jaw tightened.

"And Caleb? He didn't just steal. He broke her, likely killed her, and covered it in silence?"

Hazel nodded. "And you've survived all of it. Not by accident, but on purpose."

Autumn rose slowly, her legs stiff, her fingers clenched around the folder.

"I need to talk to Marcus."

She didn't wait for a reply. She walked outside like a woman shedding old skin. She emerged into the cool night air, still clutching the folder, her heart thudding like it wanted to outrun the truth.

As she walked, she saw a figure step out from the shadows near a parked black SUV. It was Detective Marcus King. His silhouette was familiar and steady. He took one look at her face and came toward her without a word.

"You okay?" he asked gently.

She shook her head. "No. But I'm here."

She reached for his hand without thinking, and he didn't hesitate. His palm was warm, grounding hers like a root.

"Come with me," he said softly.

* * *

In Marcus's apartment, the door shut behind them with a soft click. Autumn sank into his couch, the plush fabric embracing her like mercy. Marcus poured two glasses of red wine and set one in front of her on a nearby table. He sat beside her. Not too close, but near enough to anchor her.

"She knew, Marcus. Sam knew Caleb was dangerous. Serenity confirmed the signatures. He was the one. He *did it*."

She handed him the manila folder, her hands still trembling.

Marcus flipped it open, skimmed just enough to confirm Autumn's words, then closed it again.

"The DA's been circling him for months, and this seals it. I'll make a call."

"What about BBG?"

"That's yours, Autumn. No one can take it from you anymore."

Autumn felt a sense of relief as her body relaxed deeper into the couch. A comfortable silence settled between them.

After a few minutes, Autumn noticed Marcus fidgeting slightly, seeming stuck between his head and heart.

"I've been waiting to say something. But I needed you to have all the facts first. No blurred lines, just truth."

She blinked several times, caught off guard. "What?"

Marcus took a deep breath.

"I loved you before I even knew what to call it. A few years ago, before I was ever assigned to Sam's case, I saw you. You were speaking at that women's event she hosted. You were fire. Untouchable. I couldn't do anything then, but I never forgot."

"And now?"

"I still see you," he said. "More clearly than ever."

He stood and opened the terrace door. Autumn followed him outside, the city stretching wide beneath them.

The hum of traffic faded. Only stars and breath remained.

He leaned against the railing. "Can I ask you something?"

"You can ask me anything."

"How do you feel about me calling you Breezy?"

Autumn froze. The name hit her chest like a memory.

"Only Sam and some of my immediate family call me by that nickname."

"I know," Marcus said. "I don't want to overstep. But I think they call you that because you have something powerful in you. I know I'm not family, but if you'll let me, I'd like to call you that too."

Autumn considered his question and decided she wanted him to feel a sense of closeness to her because she felt close to him.

"I'd like that."

Their fingers intertwined like new roots from old soil.

Marcus touched her cheek before brushing back a single curl behind her ear.

"Trust me." His voice held nothing but sincerity and want.

She leaned into his touch, his warmth, his steadiness. She readied herself for his approaching lips. When hers met his, it wasn't lust, it was truth unfolding. Like breath returning to a body that had forgotten what it felt like to be safe.

When they finally pulled apart, Autumn lay her head against his shoulder, eyes fluttering closed.

"Thank you," she whispered.

"For what?" he murmured.

"For reminding me there's still hope."

Marcus smiled, tucking her close.

"There always is."

# CHAPTER SIXTEEN

# What the Mirror Won't Say

The morning light filtered softly through the diner's dusty windows, casting long shadows over the worn Formica table where Autumn sat opposite Jerald Monroe. The booth smelled of old coffee and vinyl, and the low hum of conversations and clinking dishes created a strange calm, like the world didn't know what she was about to uncover.

She slid a leather-bound flash drive across the table, her eyes locked onto his.

"When were you going to tell me about Caleb?"

Jerald didn't look up right away. His fingers circled the rim of his chipped mug, swirling cream into his coffee like it held secrets.

"She made me promise that if anything ever happened to her, I was to protect Caleb. No matter what."

Autumn leaned in, her voice tight with restraint.

"Protect him from what? Or who? Himself?"

Jerald exhaled as though the moment had aged him ten years.

"He wasn't unstable. Just...broken. Brilliant, but hollow in places no one could see. There was always something dark behind his eyes. Samantha didn't talk about it, but I knew. She was scared."

He shook his head as his words filled the space between them. Autumn stiffened. "She told me once that Caleb didn't believe in consequences. He believed everything was either inherited or owed."

Jerald reached into the inside pocket of his camel coat and slid a worn manila envelope onto the table.

"She was getting ready. Liquidating assets. Transferring power. She was planning to hand everything over to...you."

Autumn blinked. "To me? As in, Billionaire Broke Girls?"

Jerald nodded. "She believed in you even when she hated you. Especially when she hated you. She saw the future in you. But Caleb, he saw competition, and Samantha knew he wouldn't let that vision survive."

* * *

Serenity waited in the car in the diner parking lot, her fingers interlaced in silent prayer on her lap. Autumn slipped into the passenger seat, her eyes glassy, her spirit trembling under the weight of what she'd just learned.

"What if telling the truth destroys everything we've built?" Autumn asked as she settled in.

Serenity didn't flinch. Her hand reached over and rested gently on Autumn's.

"Truth doesn't destroy, it refines. Exposure doesn't kill movements, it purifies them."

"But what if it kills *him*?"

Serenity's gaze remained fixed on the road.

"Then God's justice will be done. Not ours."

Autumn closed her eyes, letting the silence hold her like a sanctuary. A fragile shift stirred inside her. Even in the darkness, mirrors could reflect grace.

Later that night, Autumn sat alone with Samantha's journal open on her lap. Her fingers traced the inked line that had been haunting her.

*Some shadows look like sons. Some sins wear your surname.*

The truth chilled her. Caleb's violence wasn't new. It was legacy. As a mother, Samantha had hidden it behind donation checks, luxury salons, and public influence. But it had always been there. Now it was hers to confront...and expose.

* * *

Rain tapped softly against the floor-to-ceiling windows as Autumn stepped into the high-rise penthouse for what would become the final time. The waters of Lake Norman rolled outside in slow, ominous waves.

Samantha sat in a pale blue robe, swirling her tea, a flicker of her former self.

"I used to think building an empire would protect me from everything," she said, not looking up. "Turns out, it made me the loneliest woman in the world."

Autumn stood at the door, arms crossed. Her guard wasn't down, not anymore.

"You didn't just build an empire, Sam. You built a prison and locked the rest of us inside."

Samantha flinched, the teacup rattling on its saucer.

"You still don't understand, do you?" her voice just above a whisper. "Everything I did, I thought I was protecting us."

"You were protecting *yourself*," Autumn replied. "From being exposed and being vulnerable."

Silence stretched between them.

Finally, Samantha looked up, eyes haunted, voice breaking.

"Promise me you'll build something better. Something honest."

Autumn hesitated, then stepped forward and placed a journal on the table. It was Samantha's old dream journal, once buried in a file cabinet, now marked with notes and grief.

"This is going to press. Not to shame you, but to show *all* of us what happens when we chase success without healing."

Samantha closed her eyes and exhaled deeply, as if releasing lifetimes of ambition and regret.

"Then let it be my confession. Let my fall become someone else's freedom."

They both welcomed the silence until Autumn couldn't hold back any longer.

"Sam, stop talking in riddles. What exactly are you saying?"

Samantha looked at her and nodded. "If I'm ever gone, don't make me a saint. Make me a mirror. So you can see what to keep, and what to heal."

# CHAPTER SEVENTEEN

# Billionaire Broke Girls

**ONE YEAR LATER**

Under the soft lavender glow of Charlotte's skyline, Autumn stood beside Marcus on the rooftop of the newly dedicated BBG Legacy House, a women's center named after Samantha Monroe, but built with Autumn's vision, faith, and healing.

On a small table behind them, Brooklyn, Serenity, and Hazel had left a circle of candles and wildflowers just in case Autumn needed to grieve, pray, or remember.

Golden light spilled over the city, not just bathing it, but blessing it.

Moments later, voices inside buzzed like electric currents. Three hundred women in denim and fuchsia filled the gold-trimmed venue. They were survivors, visionaries, dreamers. The Billionaire Broke Girls Brunch was more than an event. It was a revolution. The shimmering backdrop behind the mic read:

**BILLIONAIRE BROKE GIRLS**
**Heal Loud. Build Soft. Rise Anyway.**

Autumn stepped forward in a tailored emerald jumpsuit. Her curls crowned a face no longer dimmed by survival but ignited by purpose.

"This movement didn't come from a conference. It came from a collapse."

Her voice rang clear. Strong. Soft. Sacred.

"It was birthed after betrayal and built on the ashes of everything I thought made me worthy, like money, platforms, and friendships I thought were unshakable."

Murmurs moved through the crowd. Some nodded while others held back tears.

"My grandmother, who passed this year at 105, gave me a word. Not on a stage, but in a room full of scraps and stories."

She touched the quilt swatch in her blazer pocket.

"I was ten. I sat on the edge of her bed, watching her sew with trembling fingers. She looked at me and said, 'Don't throw away what tried to break you. Stitch it.'"

A low "Amen" came from somewhere near the front row.

"And that's what Billionaire Broke Girls is. We are not stitched with perfection, we are sewn from pain, power, and prayers."

Applause stirred like a rising tide.

"You don't have to wait until the trauma is over to begin healing. You don't need riches to be whole. You don't need to be loud to be strong. You need to believe…what hurt you still holds value."

She paused, locking eyes with the crowd.

"So today, I'm not just relaunching a brand. I'm unfolding a quilt stitched with every betrayal, every broken deal, every sacred no. And every one of you."

She lifted the quilt swatch high.

"This was sewn by a woman who buried babies and baked cakes in the same week. That's what healing is. Not forgetting but transforming."

The room thundered with applause. Some rose to their feet while others wept openly.

Brooklyn clapped with joy. Serenity bowed her head in quiet gratitude. Hazel smiled from the shadows.

In the back stood Detective Marcus with eyes full of fire and peace.

* * *

As the event came to its finale, Autumn returned to the mic as the harpist transitioned into a slow, soulful rendition of *Brown Skin Girl*.

Her voice took on a new edge—measured and unshaken.

"Before we begin the legacy funding, I have a truth to share. Not out of revenge but clarity."

The room stilled.

"We say we want legacy. But if we protect image over integrity, we rot our own roots."

Alone in a far corner in the back of the room, Caleb Monroe rose.

His gray suit hung loosely as if fleeing from his frame. He yelled through hatred as he walked up the center aisle toward the stage.

"You think she was perfect, but she wasn't! She hurt people! Controlled them! Treated love like leverage!"

Gasps. Silence. Confused stares.

"I tried to protect her legacy. But when she decided to leave it all to...*you*...to *this*," he gestured at the stage. "I couldn't let her erase me."

Autumn stepped down and approached him in the aisle.

"You didn't have to kill her."

"She chose you long before I ever touched her wine." For a moment, his mask cracked.

Hazel and Brooklyn exchanged a glance before security stepped in.

From the back, Jerald Monroe entered quietly, flanked by Marcus. Caleb didn't fight. He only lowered his head.

As they led him away, Autumn returned to the stage.

"We are not who broke us. We are not the whispers behind our backs. We are not the trauma passed down like debt. We are the ones who *rise*. And we will keep rising."

Applause. Prayers. Voices like revival.

That night, Detective Marcus showed up at Brooklyn's townhome while the ladies were debriefing the day's events.

Marcus approached Autumn. His voice was low and urgent.

"We reviewed the journals and her digital files. Caleb used her passwords. He knew she was leaving the majority to you."

Autumn's breath caught. "But he's family."

"We found fentanyl in her system and in the bottle of wine. Her prints were on the glass, but so were his. It wasn't suicide. It was a setup."

Autumn crumpled to her knees and held her face in her hands. Marcus joined her on the ground and placed her hands in his.

"You didn't lose everything. You gained clarity, and sometimes, that's where love finally finds its way in."

They didn't kiss, not yet. But their hands stayed locked as a covenant of truth.

Time passed and the air shifted. Autumn gazed out at the city skyline wondering what was next for BBG. She was so lost in her thoughts that she didn't feel Marcus come up behind her.

"I came into your life to solve a murder, but I had no idea I'd be healed by a woman who survived her own spiritual death. Autumn, you taught me how to pray again. How to breathe again. How to believe in the beauty of broken things."

She looked at him with a heart full of wishes and wonder. He was everything she knew she wanted, even at a time when wanting felt selfish and uncertain.

Marcus pulled a small black box out of his pocket and knelt in front of her.

"Autumn Brees James, will you marry me?"

Autumn's eyes filled with tears. Her voice cracked as she whispered, "Yes. A thousand times, yes!"

Brooklyn shouted. Serenity clapped. Hazel held her chest with a proud, maternal joy.

The woman who once lost everything to betrayal now stood in victory, surrounded by women who refused to break.

Billionaire Broke Girls was no longer just a movement. It was a living, breathing revolution. And it had just begun.

# The Wedding

The chandelier sparkled above the ballroom, scattering golden light across the crystal place settings and the elegant faces of guests seated in quiet reverence. The air was charged, not with spectacle, but with spirit. A sacred hush blanketed the courtyard, as if heaven leaned in to witness.

Alone in the bridal suite, Autumn stood in stillness. Her hands gently pressed against her gown as her eyes fluttered shut.

"God," she whispered, "grant me serenity to accept the things I can't change, courage to change the things I can, and wisdom to know the difference. Amen."

A soft *click* broke the silence. The door creaked open.

Music swelled in the distance. Flashes from a camera spilled into the room like sunlight.

Hazel stepped forward, her voice warm and low.

"She's ready."

Autumn stepped from the suite, her dress sweeping the floor behind her like a whispered legacy. The hallway was empty, just as Marcus had requested. Time slowed, wrapped in stillness.

At the top of the spiral staircase, she paused. Below, a sea of guests waited behind the ballroom doors. Her breath caught.

She inhaled, then descended.

Halfway down, Nadine Love appeared, her hand smoothing the six-foot train of ivory silk.

Nadine spoke softly, "Don't be nervous. You look divine. Today is yours."

Autumn adjusted the diamond pendant wrapped around her bouquet, her mother's stone, her father's promise, her own rebirth.

"Thank you. I guess I'm a little anxious."

"That just means your heart knows this is holy."

Nadine pressed the mic at her collar before turning to speak to her bridal crew. "Alright, everyone. Our bride is on the move."

The grand double doors opened.

Gasps and camera shutters filled the room.

Autumn stepped into view, bathed in golden light. Her eyes scanned the crowd. Serenity. Brooklyn. Hazel. The fierce women of Billionaire Broke Girls, all standing in solidarity, in color-blocked gowns, tear-streaked and proud.

Waiting at the altar with a calm strength in his eyes that met hers across every battle, every doubt, was Marcus.

Halfway down the aisle, Autumn paused, steadying her breath. Once in position, she nodded to Hazel, who was officiating the ceremony.

"The couple has prepared vows to read aloud."

Autumn turned to Marcus, bouquet trembling in her hands.

"Marcus, you walked into my life when everything felt like it was falling apart. But somehow, you didn't try to fix me. You just stood close. Quiet enough for me to hear God again. Before I knew your name, I dreamt of your spirit. You were the bridge in my wilderness. The calm in my unraveling. I used to believe love was something to earn. Something that left when the spotlight faded. Something that broke me before it held me. But you, you loved me into wholeness. You saw the girl in ashes and called forth the woman with purpose. I vow to never forget the altar God built between us. I vow to cover you in prayer before I ever cover you in expectations. I vow to listen, not just with my ears, but with my soul. I vow to choose you in every storm and celebrate you in every sunrise. And when life breaks wide open, I vow to meet you there, in the rubble, with faith in one hand, and your hand in the other. Loving you isn't the end of my story. It's the chapter where I finally learned I was worthy of God's best, which is exactly what you are."

The room exhaled. Marcus stepped closer, his voice deep and firm.

"Autumn, you didn't just walk into my life, you interrupted it. With fire and favor. With a testimony that turned my quiet faith into a wild belief. You challenged my silence and turned it into a sanctuary. I've seen the weight you've carried, including overcoming betrayals that should've buried you. But you never stopped choosing to walk in your purpose. That's when I knew you weren't just the love of my life, you were the assignment of my soul. Today, I vow to be your safe space when the world grows loud. I vow to intercede when you're too tired to pray. To protect your name in rooms you're not in. To wash your feet when your spirit feels weary. I vow to never confuse your strength with not needing support. I will stand behind you when you lead, beside you when you build, and in front of you when you need covering. You taught me that legacy isn't built in bank accounts. It's built in the way we love, and the way we lift. Autumn, I don't just love you. I respect you. I believe in you. I vow never to stop choosing you, even when life tries to make us forget why we started. You're not just my wife. You're my witness to how far God can take a man who finally surrenders."

Marcus gently wiped a tear from Autumn's cheek as they held one another's gaze.

After a second of blinking to pull back her own tears, Hazel proceeded with the ceremony, offering a bit of comic relief.

"Detective Marcus LaVelle King, do you promise to love Autumn with truth, tenderness, and tequila when needed?"

Marcus laughed and answered, "With my whole soul."

"Autumn Brees James, do you vow to build altars, not platforms, and leave room for grace when things fall apart?"

Autumn smiled through tears.

"Every day with every breath."

"With the power vested in me by the state of North Carolina, I now pronounce..."

Autumn heard nothing else as she found herself in an embrace with the man she would love for a lifetime.

Their kiss was not just a symbol. It was a sentence.

A sealing.

A *beginning*.

* * *

Later that evening, beneath glittering chandeliers and surrounded by loved ones, Autumn sat quietly. Marcus danced with her niece across the floor. Serenity passed slices of cake. Hazel toasted with Brooklyn. Laughter rang through the room. Autumn wanted to remember the moment forever.

She looked up as Marcus lifted her hand into his.

"This is just the beginning."

She smiled as she rested her head against his chest. She was no longer just a survivor. She was a queen crowned by grace. It was time to write a new legacy. One of faith, resilience, fierce love, and a billionaire spirit born not from riches...but from healing.

# The Mirror and the Mantle

## One Year Later

The sunlight entered through the glass-paneled atrium of the Harvey B. Gantt Center, bathing everything it touched in warmth. Inside, heels clicked with purpose, babies gurgled in carriers, and the quiet rustle of journals being opened filled the space with expectancy.

Autumn stood backstage in a soft pink blazer, no shoulder pads, no shapewear, no earpiece buzzing commands. She didn't need to be edited anymore. She had become the unfiltered version of herself.

The second annual *Billionaire Broke Girls Brunch* was officially sold out. Not because of influencer campaigns or SEO funnels, but because when women get free, they tell the truth, and truth travels.

The banners that framed the room bore bold, layered imagery. Mosaic portraits of fractured faces pieced together in stained-glass patterns of survival. Logos that hinted at the divine feminine and sacred fire, each one centered on strength, healing, and unity. There wasn't a celebrity speaker or headliner. The faces on the wall *were* the movement.

Brooklyn stood at the back, holding a clipboard she didn't need, whispering instructions to no one. She beamed like a big sister at graduation.

Hazel, regal in a flowing indigo wrap dress, nodded toward Serenity who wore linen and locs like a prophetess.

Autumn stepped into the spotlight, the crowd humming into silence as her heels clicked across the polished floor. She didn't rush. She didn't apologize. She took the mic like it was her mantle.

"Last year, I stood before you with shaking hands and a broken heart. I thought healing was a destination. But now I know, it's a daily walk. A rhythm. A release."

Heads bowed. Shoulders shook.

"I used to think my worth was in what I built—my title, my bank account, my boardroom. But now I know it's in what I *surrendered.*

My identity wasn't stolen when the company fell apart. It was *revealed.*"

She reached beneath the podium and pulled out a small, cracked mirror, the kind that once sat on a glossy corner desk.

"This mirror hung in my old office. Every morning I checked it to make sure I looked powerful, so no one could see how broken I really was. But now? I hang it in my home as a reminder..."

Her voice softened, thick with tears.

"Flawed can still flourish."

The crowd erupted. Snaps. *Amens.* Hands lifted in freedom.

At each place setting, linen napkins were folded into lotus shapes. Embroidered on each was the statement:

Legacy Looks Like Healing in Public

The napkin wave began. Not for appetizers or champagne toasts, but as a resurrection cry, a victory dance at tables once built to exclude them.

Brooklyn led the chant from the side. "This ain't no brunch. It's a *birthing room!*"

Autumn let the moment wash over her.

"You can lose the job, the man, the house, the reputation," she said, her voice trembling. "But if you find your soul? Baby, you've found *everything*."

Later that night, the stars hung like witnesses above the city. Autumn stood barefoot on the terrace wrapped in Marcus's arms, her heels forgotten near the doorway. Anita Baker's voice hummed through hidden speakers.

They swayed together under the velvet sky.

"Do you ever regret walking away from it all?" Marcus asked, his voice low and reverent.

Autumn rested her cheek against his chest, her fingers curled softly at his back.

"Not for a second," she whispered. "Because I didn't walk away from something, I walked *toward myself*."

She looked up, eyes bright. "Now? I'm walking toward forever."

He kissed her forehead and held her tighter.

Autumn's fingers traced the cracked mirror again, now tucked beneath her arm like a final chapter. She looked out at the sky.

"I kept my promise, God."

She turned back to the light, to the music, to the love. To the movement that now carried its own momentum. She had inherited more than a story. She had inherited a mantle. One she wore unafraid.

As the sky opened wide with stars, a new chapter began. Not just in her story, but in the story of every woman who finally believed she could be both **healed and held.**

# About the Author

Sharain Hemingway is a dynamic storyteller, speaker, and spiritual disruptor whose words heal as much as they provoke. Born and raised in the soul-stirring sands of Myrtle Beach, South Carolina, Sharain is a proud graduate of North Myrtle Beach High School and Winthrop University, where her passion for people, faith, and truth began to sharpen.

Sharain is a 2x published author who writes with the grit of a woman who has lived through betrayal, brokenness, and breakthrough, and dares to speak what many only whisper. *Billionaire Broke Girls* is more than a book. It's a movement. A mirror. A mantle. It explores what happens when powerful women crumble in private but rise in purpose anchored not in performance, but in healing.

Sharain's passion for this story was born from her own journey of losing everything she thought mattered: title, trust, and identity, only to discover the treasure in truth. Through each character, she explores generational trauma, spiritual awakening, emotional intelligence, and the power of sisterhood as sacred medicine.

As an emerging literary voice for this generation of faith-filled, soul-tired women, Sharain is committed to writing stories that don't just entertain but deliver. Her work holds space for Black women to be both soft and strong, spiritual and strategic, broken and still worthy.

When she's not writing, Sharain is mentoring young women, golfing, and building her next wave of stories that center truth, transparency, and transformation.

*To learn more, visit www.RainReview222.com.*

# Q&A with Sharain Hemingway

**Q: Why did you feel the need to publish *Billionaire Broke Girls* at a time like this, culturally, spiritually, and personally?**

*A: I felt a deep urgency. We're in a season where women are breaking down behind closed doors while being applauded publicly. Culturally, we glorify hustle and silence healing. Spiritually, God called me to expose how performance and platforms have replaced purpose. Personally, I was healing, and I wanted to write from that raw, in-between place to remind women they're not alone.*

**Q: What does the title *Billionaire Broke Girls* really mean?**

*A: It's about the paradox. You can be rich in ambition but bankrupt in identity. You can own businesses but be broke in boundaries. It's about redefining wealth from the inside out, where healing, faith, and sisterhood are currency.*

**Q: Who is this book for?**

*A: For the woman who has survived betrayal, who's rebuilt herself in silence, who knows how to succeed but not how to rest. For the dreamer, the doer, the one holding everyone else together but falling apart quietly. Ages 18 to 98, this is your invitation to heal aloud.*

**Q: What does Autumn's character reveal about high-functioning grief?**

*A: Autumn is the poster child for silent suffering. She shows us what it means to look "put together" while unraveling internally. Her journey teaches us that healing doesn't mean fixing. It means finally being honest with ourselves.*

**Q: What spiritual battle does Autumn face that readers might relate to?**

*A: She confuses discernment with distrust. She's loyal to dysfunction because she was trained to ignore her gut. Many of us were raised to submit to titles instead of truth, and Autumn's journey breaks that spiritual stronghold.*

**Q: How does Brooklyn's character represent sacred sisterhood?**

*A: Brooklyn is the friend who won't let you quit. She shows up with ginger tea and tough love. She teaches us that healing isn't always pretty, but it's powerful when done in community.*

**Q: Hazel is a lawyer, but also a spiritual anchor. What's her role in the healing arc?**

*A: Hazel teaches that legal boundaries are spiritual ones too. She represents order, accountability, and wisdom. She's the reminder that healing includes contracts, consequences, and clarity.*

**Q: Serenity is a therapist, but also a prophet in disguise. What makes her unique?**

*A: Serenity holds space for both scripture and science. She doesn't push healing, she partners with it. Her spiritual intuition challenges us to confront the cravings beneath our chaos.*

**Q: Caleb's character carries a dark twist. What does his mindset reveal?**

*A: Caleb shows us what unhealed sonship can become. His resentment wasn't about money, it was about feeling invisible. He represents generational pain left unchecked. His story is a cautionary tale about ignoring emotional inheritance.*

**Q: Samantha Monroe is both villain and victim. What was her internal war?**

*A: Samantha built an empire on fear disguised as empowerment. She was a woman so desperate not to fail that she weaponized love. Her journal reveals a late repentance, proof that people can be broken and still prophetic.*

**Q: What does "broke" mean in the context of this book?**

*A: Broke isn't just about money. It's about spiritual bankruptcy, emotional depletion, and identity theft. But it's also the breaking before the breakthrough.*

**Q: What's the role of prophetic dreams in the novel?**

*A: Dreams in the book represent God's whisper when we're too exhausted to hear Him. They're roadmaps from the Spirit to help the characters and readers navigate the unseen battles.*

**Q: How does the book challenge traditional definitions of success?**

*A: It exposes how success without surrender is still suffering. We see women with followers, money, and titles, but no peace. Real success is when you can sleep at night and not perform for love.*

**Q: There's a strong theme of betrayal. How do you want readers to process their own betrayals through this story?**

*A: I want them to realize that betrayal is often the doorway to purpose. It doesn't destroy you, it reveals who's not meant to walk into your next chapter. Healing begins when we release the need for closure and trust God for justice.*

**Q: If readers only remember one scene, which do you hope it is?**

*A: The moment Autumn reads Sam's journal and sees her own anointing through her betrayer's eyes. That scene reminds us that sometimes the people who hurt us saw our greatness and feared it.*

**Q: What do you hope women feel when they finish the last page?**

*A: Seen. Heard. Called. Not for performance, but for purpose. I want them to put the book down and pick up their journal, their faith, their business plan, or their boundary list.*

**Q: What does "Build from the Bones" mean as a chapter title and a lifestyle?**

*A: It means starting over with what's left after the fire. Not pretending it didn't happen, but building a holy life from the ashes. Bones are what remain after death. They're sacred and structural. That's where we begin.*

**Q: Why did you end the story with a wedding and a brunch?**

*A: The wedding represents a personal covenant. The brunch represents public calling. Together, they symbolize wholeness: love, legacy, and leadership rooted in healing.*

**Q: What scripture or quotes, if any, shaped this book the most?**

*A: Isaiah 61:3: "To give them beauty for ashes, the oil of joy for mourning, the garment of praise for the spirit of heaviness." This story is about scripture with lashes, laptops, and luxury linen.*